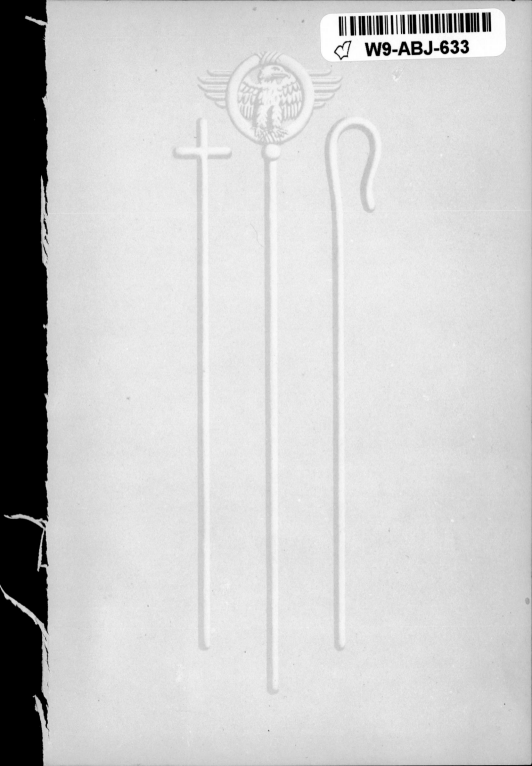

THE QUEST

THE

CONCORDIA PUBLISHINGHOUSE

QUEST

The Story of the Shepherds of Bethlehem

By LUDWIG BAUER

Saint Louis — 1945

DEDICATED TO THE LOVE
OF CHRIST, MY SAVIOR,
BY A SINNER SAVED
BY GRACE

Contents

THE QUEST

THE QUEST

I

Asa the Shepherd

THE rays of the morning sun were warming the back of old Asa as he stood leaning on his staff of cedar wood, with both hands wrapped around the smooth and time-worn crook, his bearded chin resting on the back of the uppermost hand. Deep-set brown eyes, almost hidden under shaggy white-haired brows, shone in rapture as they gazed over the valley. A crumpled old felt hat, a veteran of endless fights with wind and weather, afforded but slight protection against the burning sun. A time-worn lambskin, its fur rubbed off in spots, covered the slender hips and brown-skinned shoulder, while down over his back hung a woolen plaid, its threadbare condition telling of years of faithful service. Wooden sandals, fastened with soft brown pieces of leather to corded, strong-muscled legs, made up the simple outfit of the herder. The corners of his eyes were lined with tiny crow's-feet and were puckered from the habit of gazing into great distances under the rays of a glistening sun. A soft white beard, that needed combing, hid a well-proportioned mouth and jaw. His prominent nose told that he was of Jewish origin. And old Asa was proud of this. A spark of pride would always grace his features whenever he was called by that name.

Asa was a dreamer, and his occupation gave him ample opportunity to develop and nourish his dreams. Into his eyes came an expression of sadness as he viewed the valley of his nativity. On his right towards the east lay the ancient town of Bethlehem, its terraced gardens and vineyards basking

in the golden noonday sun; covering the floor of the valley
were the fertile fields of Boaz and Ruth, the blessed ancestors
of King David. A sea of golden-ripe wheat swayed in ripples
to the gentle touch and play of the wind, expressing to the
eye of the herder the beauty that framed the valley.

It was not the first time that Asa had beheld the beauty
of the fields. No, he was born and reared in the valley. But
whenever he gazed over it, he would dream of the boy that
grew up to become a mighty king and a deliverer of his
people. He would see him as a little boy at play with his
sheep and watch him grow to manhood. He would go along
at his side to battle with the mighty enemy and see him
returning a hero, a conqueror of his foe. To think and dream
of David the King and of the former greatness of his people
had become an obsession with him.

Being slightly cramped in his present position, he lifted
his head and began to walk a few steps toward his sheep,
which were untiringly cropping their food from the hillside,
covered scantily with grass.

A big woolly-haired sheepdog came bounding up to lick
the gnarled hand of the herder, who began to talk to him.
Between them there seemed complete unity and understanding. The dog was one of those animals whose ancestry could
only be guessed at; in other words, a mongrel. But as it
frequently happens, dogs of this kind very often possess the
fine points of a thoroughbred. Caleb was this kind of dog.
The body and form was that of a collie, but the sharp,
pointed muzzle and the small head, together with the thick,
heavy brown fur that covered the neck and breast, suggested
that he was predominantly sheep dog. To the old herder he
was both servant and loyal friend. Together they had with-
stood many storms and hardships.

Asa's eyes rested on a magnificent building situated on the

summit of a hill southeast of Bethlehem. It was the Fortress Palace of King Herod the Great. From the top of its towers one could view the highland wilderness of Judea, and the eye could follow for many miles the contours of the caravan road which led to Hebron. The palace was indeed a marvel of architectural beauty, with all the surrounding buildings of Herod's courtiers and the quarters of his mixed army of mercenaries. A gleam of hate, mingled with something akin to sorrow, came into the eyes of the old herder as he expressed his thoughts aloud to the dog lying at his feet.

"Just look, Caleb!" he said. "How beautiful yonder palace is, wrought by the sweat and blood of my brethren, who were forced to serve this dog of an Idumean! He, the tyrant, calls himself Herod the Great. Bah! Cursed be he, the murderer of wife and sons, the spittle-licker of the mighty in the accursed Rome!"

Asa was fully aware of the growing influence of the life and conversation of the Romans over his people, and his quick and active mind resented it. He knew that the hearts of the majority of his people ached with him. But they were helpless to check this influence, especially so because of the misguidance of their spiritual leaders, the Sanhedrin. Many of its members were bought by the Romans, and others became willing tools to work the wily schemes of the cunning Herod. The sacred office of the high priest, around which centered the life and hope of the people, had become the seat of greediness and politics, and was occupied by a creature chosen by Herod.

Moisture filled the eyes of the herder as these thoughts passed through his mind, and pain constricted his voice as he mumbled aloud the cry, "Oh, for the glory of Israel, which is departed from my people!"

The sun began to sink low in the west, but to Asa this

mattered little. His eyes were still clinging to the dust-covered road below him. This was a much traveled road of late. An edict had come from Rome, demanding a census of all the people of Israel. Herod willingly consented to the demand, only too glad to grant a favor to the mighty Caesar, under whose good will he was able to remain on the throne of Judea.

But fearing the displeasure of the people, Herod agreed that the census should be made in the Jewish method of registration, not in the Roman method, counting each individual town and city, as was done at the present. According to the Jewish law a census could be taken by counting only the members of each of the Twelve Tribes, which meant that each member should go to the place from which he originated. This was the reason for the many travelers on the road. Asa had seen them for many days; groups of two or three people; larger groups of men, women, and their children coming from the town of Bethlehem on their way to the Holy City; and many others coming from the crowded city to seek rest and comfort in the coolness of the village inn. A long train of camels, their backs laden with various kinds of merchandise, came over a little rise of the dust-clouded road, plodding patiently on to their destination, paying scant attention to the cries and gesticulations of their brown-skinned drivers.

II

The Two Calebs

IT was only after the caravan had entered and disappeared into Bethlehem that Asa centered his eyes again upon the rest of the travelers, and as he did so, he spied the figure of a horseman galloping around a sharp bend in the road. "This fellow certainly rides the spurs," he said to himself as he beheld the animal covered with sweat. A wild rage against the rider took possession of him as he saw the lead-loaded stock of the horsewhip descend on the head of the spirited animal, which was willing but too tired to move faster. The sight of the brutal treatment angered Asa. His right hand came up with fist clenched, while his left hand grasped the formidable staff, shaking it in helpless rage at the horseman.

And as the rider drew close, Asa's anger found an outlet as he exclaimed, "I might have known; only a creature from the palace could do such a thing! The scarlet cloak and the tunic tell me that he hails from that nest of iniquity. Oh, were I twenty years younger, I would put this staff to good use and give this dog the punishment he deserves!"

Just then Caleb came into action. The dog had been lying peacefully at Asa's feet, snoozing. But suddenly, at the sound of Asa's voice, he jumped up with a snarl and flew like an arrow straight for the horse and rider, a few hundred yards beyond him, madly barking. The horseman became aware of the furious dog and attempted to run him down. But he did not succeed, for the dog had already jumped toward the horse and rider with open mouth and vicious

teeth. Only through the unexpected action of the horse did
the dog miss his aim. The horse, terror-stricken by the sudden
attack of the dog, reared, its front legs beating the air. Un-
prepared, the rider fell from the horse into the dust of the
road. Asa was breathless as he reached the snarling dog.
"Hush, Caleb!" he said. "Get back and be still! Where are
your manners?"

Grasping the dog by the neck, he succeeded in pulling
him off the dust-covered rider. But a mad growl continued
to come from the dog as he kept watching the soldier.

"Be quiet, Caleb!" the old herder soothed. "You have done
enough evil. I shall try to seek forgiveness for your behavior,
if it pleases the gentleman to grant it."

But a bright gleam of satisfaction, which shone for a fleeting
moment in the old man's eyes, belied his words. The old
herder was really pleased as he looked upon the bedraggled
figure, but his pleasure lasted but for a moment, for the
thrown horseman had quickly collected his wits. Pulling his
cloak closer around his body with his left hand and grasping
hard with the fingers of his right hand the ivory hilt of a
dagger, he advanced toward Asa and thus addressed him
angrily, "Your impudence is greater than the mad fury of
this dog. How dare you address me before I give you leave
to do so!"

Taken by surprise at hearing the angry words, Asa looked
away from his dog into the face of the proud courtier and
replied in an even voice, "I have not addressed or spoken
to you, O proud Herodian. Your ears have deceived you."

A loud peal of laughter was heard when Asa uttered these
words. It came from a small group of travelers who had
stopped for a while by the wayside to watch the outcome of
the unusual affair. Ignoring the group, the rider, with a
haughty, scornful glance from his beady eyes, said to the

shepherd with a snarl, pulling the dagger from his belt, "You miserable wretch! For these words I shall have your life! Mine ears have heard you say, 'Be quiet, Caleb!' and yet you dare to lie."

A trace of a smile crept for a moment over the corners of Asa's mouth as he listened to the soldier's reply, and he answered, "May I humbly request your name, O Herodian?"

Some of the anger and hate began to leave the face of the soldier as he was thus addressed. He did not see the barb in the old herder's question as he replied, "Your request is granted. I am known as Captain Caleb from the household of our most gracious King Herod."

After making this reply, Captain Caleb glanced expectantly at Asa and the little group of wayfarers, hoping to see them stricken with fear. But a sickening surprise swept over him as the shout "Kill the Idumean dog!" came to his sensitive ears. Fear crept into the heart of the captain. But it was Asa who unknowingly took away the attention of the travelers from the cowering soldier as he answered, "I thank you, O Herodian, for granting my humble request, and I assure you I shall be more careful in the future in calling the name of my dog Caleb in the presence of your so noble person. I fear the dog might not like it."

The soldier's mad fury, as he found himself thus referred to, was drowned by the hilarity coming from the bystanders. His small hate-filled eyes, glancing over the group, could read satisfaction and something akin to challenge in their threatening look. This made the blood mount higher in his otherwise bloodless cheeks. The Herodian, however, by nature a cautious fellow, knew when it was wise to be careful. For he saw that in the group there was more than one man who could match him in strength and bravery. At heart a coward, he was brave only when the odds were in his favor.

For a moment his eyes rested longingly on the powerful battlements of the palace only a few miles distant from where he stood, and he could not help thinking how a small handful of the mercenaries, who were his to command, could now be of great service to him.

Noting the hesitation of the captain and reading his thoughts correctly, Asa deemed it wise to apologize.

"I meant no insult, sir," he said, "and if it gives you any satisfaction, I humbly ask your forgiveness for the action of my dog. He is a gentle animal, and I cannot understand his dislike for your person, for I am sure he has never laid eyes on you before."

In this Asa was mistaken. The soldier could have shown the old man two deep scars on his right wrist, evidently from the teeth of this dog. But instead of showing them to Asa, the courtier asked rather tardily, "Have you a son by the name of David?"

"Yes, sir, this I have," the herder replied proudly and with warmth. "But why, may I ask, do you want to know?"

For reasons unknown to Asa, the Herodian snapped cuttingly, "This, my friend, is for you to find out. But remember and listen carefully. Caleb, the Idumean, will not forget the mocking sneers at the expense of his person. I shall pay you back in full some day!"

With this threat to the old Jew, Caleb stepped to the side of his horse, which had come to a stand a few yards away, grateful for the chance to rest. But it was only with difficulty that he grasped the trailing reins and mounted the still nervous animal. With a last look of deadly hatred at Asa and the dog, he drove in the spurs and quickly rode off.

For a long time old Asa stood motionless, his eyes following the form of the fast disappearing rider; then he moved with a slow, heavy step to the side of his dog, whom he found busily licking a wound on his right front leg. The old herder, not knowing that the dog was hurt, bent quickly over him, to find, with relief, that there was nothing serious. Only an abrasion of the skin, no bones broken.

One of the bystanders, a dark-visaged, burly trader from near-by Jericho, came closer and looked down at the dog, who in turn looked at him with inquiring eyes. Asa seemed to take no notice of this, until the man spoke.

"Friend," he said, "if your ear is open to the advice of an honest man, take this from me, and leave this place at once. This Idumean dog wills you no good."

Asa looked up into the speaker's face and, feeling it to be an honest one, replied with a winning smile, "I am grateful to you for your kind words. But as to my leaving this place only because I offended, and that not without just cause, the vanity and pride of one from that cursed place," pointing with a gnarled finger in the direction of the castle, "this I will not do! I have grown old with yonder fields and valley, and by the Great Jehovah's mercy I expect to be buried there when my time comes!"

"From your lips come true but unwise words," the trader nodded, shaking his head, "for you will be buried there, if you remain in this location, for I happen to know this infidel better than you. He is a fiend. Do not ask me how I know, but if you have any doubt as to how he avenges an insult, let your eyes rest for a moment on this."

With these words the trader exposed his two hands (or, we should rather say, his two thumbless hands, with all their fingers maimed and broken). Asa stared at the maimed hands and with a visible tightening of his throat muscles asked, "How in the name of heaven did you come by this?"

"How I was robbed of my thumbs and of the use of my two good hands, my friend, is a long story," the trader replied. "But as you are unwilling to leave this valley, for the safety of your life, so was I once unwilling to give up the honor of my daughter, just so that I could go free and unharmed."

Respect for the burly trader from Jericho flamed up in the herder's eyes. He suppressed his emotion, however, to inquire further of the man's sorrow.

"I would not have shown you this," the trader continued, "but there rises pity in my heart for you. Your steadfast refusal to leave the valley influenced me to show you that dog's evil work. For this fiend will have little respect for those gray hairs of yours."

The sincerity of the crippled merchant was apparent to Asa, who desired to learn more about him and to know him better. But in response to Asa's invitation to share bread and salt with him at the sheep camp, only a half mile distant, the man from Jericho told him that his business in Bethlehem was very pressing, but that he would gladly accept the invitation on his return trip to Jericho. The two men then parted.

Very slowly the old herder walked back up the hill with Caleb, who limped along behind on three legs. His mind was still filled with the events that had happened so recently. The more he thought about them, the more enraged he became. "A curse on this mangy cur!" he spat aloud. "Who is he to call me, who am a free man, a miserable wretch?"

His turbulent thoughts forced him to a stop, made him lift his eyes into the purple sky of the evening, as if to seek help and comfort from his Creator above. "God of my fathers, take not from me the hope of Thy promised Messiah," he prayed.

Great sorrow was evident from this outburst of emotion coming from the lips of the old herder.

Reaching the camp, which consisted of a little mud hut, in which the sheepherders found protection against the chill of the nights, Asa entered the hut and reappeared with a small wooden basin filled with water. Under his left arm he held a small, dark-colored case. Placing both the basin and the case on the ground before him, he hunched down beside the dog. Seeming to sense his master's good intention, the dog began to lick his hand. Asa, more from habit than from any fixed purpose, expressed his thoughts aloud to the dog.

"Yes, and this I know, my Caleb," he said, "I do not blame you for your action against this infidel; but I would be less worried if you could tell me the reason for it. Now hold still, until I finish." And, as if the dog understood his master's words, he submitted willingly to the cleansing and treatment of the wound. Pouring the water on the ground after he had cleansed the wound thoroughly, Asa set the basin beside him and opened the lid of the box. He took out a white strip of linen, spread it on the flat of his bended knee, and applied with a horn spoon a brownish looking ointment on the surface of the cloth. After placing the salve and spoon back into the box, he bound the injured leg of the dog and fastened the linen securely. As Asa was thus occupied, he continued to converse with himself. He could not forget the look of hatred in the eyes of the Idumean as he left, and he worried not a little about it.

"Why did he ask me if I had a son by the name of David?" Asa mused. "David, my son, must have had some business with this dog before, and I have a notion that it was not to the Herodian's advantage. I wish I knew. But David, I know, can be very closemouthed." Determination for a moment crossed his old face as he continued, "But I shall find the reason thereof when my son returns from Bethlehem."

Bidding the dog remain in the shadow of the silvery-crowned olive trees that surrounded the camp, Asa walked over to his flock. The sun in the western sky was a red ball of fire, and as the noonday heat began to ebb, a refreshing breeze blew from over the distant wilderness of Judea. Gazing into the distance, he could make out another herd of sheep, advancing slowly toward the road from the direction of the ancient city of Jericho, led by Nathan, his kinsman. A few hundred feet from the camp were the sheepfolds in which the flocks were kept for the night and which were used as a protection against mountain lions and other prowling marauders. With his flock safely in the enclosure, Asa fastened the gate by winding a leather loop around the gate post. He then returned to the hut to prepare the evening meal. Just as he had finished cooking the food, Nathan, his kinsman, entered, and after Asa had given thanks for the meal, both men sat down and ate in silence.

The young herder, noticing the bandaged leg of the dog lying before the fire, asked Asa the cause of the injury. Asa seemed to ignore the question.

"Do you know Caleb, the Idumean?" Asa asked.

The giant form of Nathan became erect, and, forgetting the meal, he looked wonderingly at the old man.

"Why this question?" he asked in return.

As no answer came to his question, he remarked dryly, "Yea, I do. Who does not? For do not his evil deeds cry for vengeance from the very housetops and proclaim him as the satanic tool of the tyrant?" Then, glancing at the sleeping dog, he asked, "But what about Caleb? What happened to him?"

Asa related the event of the day, then voiced the feeling that now filled his heart and mind.

"Does David, my son, know him? Have the two met before?" he asked.

Nathan saw the anxiety in the old herder's eyes and felt sorry. Yet he could not tell the truth to him without breaking a sacred promise to David.

"This, O Asa, I cannot tell you. You must ask David about that," he answered.

The old man's persistence was in vain, since Nathan would tell him no more. They finished their meal in silence; then, rising from the table, they seated themselves before the hut, awaiting the return of David from Bethlehem.

III

David Becomes a Proud Father

AVID, the only son of old Asa, had left the sheep camp early in the morning to visit his bride-wife, who was about to become a mother. With a gay, happy step he neared the town. Pearly drops of morning dew glistened in his mass of black hair, reaching in natural waves to the base of his sturdy neck. An old felt hat, secured with a chin strap, dangled over a pair of broad shoulders. The manner of his dress marked him as a man of the hills and the out-of-doors. A white linen cloth girded his loins. Over this was a piece of white lambskin, which extended over his left shoulder, thus exposing the right part of the chest and shoulder to wind and weather. On his right hip he carried a flask of tooled leather, filled with wine or some mixture prepared of wild honey and water. His right hand gripped the shaft of a stout sheepherder's staff. Muscular legs supported a superbly built body. His sandaled feet moved rhythmically through the ankle-deep dust of the road, and a pair of clear brown eyes expressed the vigor and joy he felt in anticipation of the coming reunion with his wife; and evident in the smooth and sunburnt face, with the aquiline nose, was utter tranquillity and peace of mind.

The first rays of the morning sun were creeping over the housetops as David viewed the ancient town with something akin to worship. Ah, how he loved it! It had been for centuries the home and dwelling place of his ancestors. Up the terraced hill with its dew-covered gardens his steps led on, until he reached the summit of the gray ridge upon which the town was built.

Before him was situated the village inn, or khan. Despite the early morning hours, the occupants of the inn were up and busy, preparing for departure to Jerusalem. But David's feet were hurrying past the structure, ignoring the desire to watch the loading of the camels lying in a long line before the khan. After entering the town proper, he turned his footsteps toward a gently rising slope, on which nestled his home under the shadow of a grove of olive trees. The walls of the cottage glistened white in the soft rays of the morning sun as David listened to the cooing of the doves on the housetop. Stepping up to the entrance, he took off his travel-stained sandals, leaving them beside his hat and staff, paused for a moment on the straw mat at the door and then entered the house. He found that Elizabeth, his wife, was not alone. An old neighbor, named Lea, was attending her, and to his ears came the protesting cry of a newborn babe.

Like a man in a trance David started toward the bed on which his wife was lying under gayly colored quilts. As their eyes met, she reassured him with a contented smile, and a great happiness shone in her eyes as she looked up to him. He dropped to his knees beside the bed and whispered, "Is — is everything all right, my beloved?"

He looked into her happy eyes and saw the nod of her head. His joy was overwhelming. He continued excitedly, "My dear! Am I the father of a son or a daughter?"

In answer to his question, Elizabeth lifted one end of the warm quilts, whereupon David beheld the little red body of an infant boy. Long and intently did the young father look upon his first-born. Reluctantly taking his eyes off the babe, he lifted them toward the heavens, his lips moving in silent prayer of thanks to God for this gift of a son.

The old woman who had stood silently beside the couple

left the room to prepare refreshments for David, leaving the pair to their joy and happiness. Again and again David looked at his son lying close beside the warm body of the happy mother. And like any young couple with their first-born, David and Elizabeth made plans for the child's future. Listening to the tender voice of his wife, David was greatly surprised when Elizabeth told him that their son was born under the sign of a star. She turned the tiny body of her little son so that his father could see a small star the size of a man's fingernail between the tiny shoulder blades of the infant. He was awed as he beheld the mark, and a strong feeling grew within him that this mark would have a great influence over the life of the child. But he spoke no word of this to the young mother.

Lea, the midwife and neighbor, returned to the room with a tray of food, depositing it on the painted surface of a table which stood in the center of the large room. She then poured water over the hands of the young herder into a brazen basin from a brazen ewer which she took from a ledge that ran along the wall. David washed his hands before he partook of the meal of boiled rice and stewed fruits. After he had finished eating, he again washed his hands, and then sat beside his wife's bed.

The hours flew by far too rapidly for the happy pair. Lea had returned to her own home to do her chores, but promised to return before very long. Alone, they talked for some time. Their young son was the only subject of their conversation. The name to be given to him was a matter of immediate concern to them. After discussing many names as suitable for the young child, they finally decided on the name Jonathan, meaning "a gift of God." The proud father conse-crated the choice of the name with the words "He surely will bring much honor to this name, just as the son of the mighty

Saul once brought honor to it for his posterity."

Eventide had now drawn near. A cool, refreshing breeze began to blow over the heat-weary town. David was reluctant to leave. He wanted to fulfill his wife's unspoken desire for him to remain for the night. But he felt that he should go, for his old father was expecting him back at the sheep camp. Soon afterwards he left with the promise to return the next day.

I V

David and Marcus

URRYING along the road toward his father's camp, David was humming the joy of his breast into the cool breeze of the evening as he breathed with rapture the aroma coming from the clusters of anemones that grew along the edge of the road. David's love for the valley and the land where he was born shone in the bright glance of his eyes. Every bush and tree that grew on the gentle slopes seemed to greet him as an old friend. Despite his youth (David was twenty-two years of age) he knew and had experienced the misrule of his beloved land by the ruthless hand of a Herod. It was not so much the thought of being subjected to a Roman that made him feel so bitter; it was rather the servile attitude of a Herod to the mighty Caesar that made him despise the Idumean.

David was about to enter a gorge that led to his father's camp, when he saw a troop of horsemen come into view around the bend of the road. The last rays of the sun, disappearing over the rim of the western horizon, were reflected in a flash from the armor and burnished helmets of the riders. Like the wind they swept towards him, ignoring the curses and clenched fists from road-weary travelers who happened along the road.

David's eyes were glued on the face of the foremost rider, apparently the leader. And as soon as he recognized the man, he exclaimed, "Marcus the Centurion!"

Almost abreast of the young herder, the rider pulled his sweating mount to a stop, raising a cloud of dust as the rest of his followers lined up behind him. Gracefully swinging his right leg over the rump of his mount, he came out of the saddle and exclaimed, "By the great Pollus, if it isn't my friend David! And how are you?"

Sincere pleasure and surprise mingled in the Roman's words of greeting as he pressed the hand of David and said, "Surely many months have passed since I had the pleasure of beholding your face."

Into David's eyes crept a gleam of joy as he warmly replied, "I thank you, O Marcus, for deeming me worthy of being remembered in your heart, and I rejoice in seeing you."

"Come, come, my good David, why so humble? Why should I not remember you?" the Roman laughed. "Do I not owe my life to you and your father? How is your worthy father?"

The young herder, somewhat self-conscious in the presence of the noble Roman, replied, "My father is well and will be glad to hear from you. But we thought you were at Damascus with the good Silvanus."

"And so I was," the Roman replied smiling slightly, evidently not disposed to explain at this time his return from Damascus. David understood quickly. He thought he knew why the Roman garrison was strengthened, for new trouble was brewing between his people and the oppressor. The thought brought to his clear brown eyes a flicker of pain, which, however, disappeared when the conversation turned to his own family.

When David told the listening rider of the birth of his son, he saw a trace of sadness come over the fine-cut features of his friend, but declined to ask the reason therefor.

Night was drawing near, and both men were anxious to be gone. As they bade each other good-by, Marcus promised the proud father to see his son as soon as time would allow him to do so.

At the Camp

WHEN David arrived at the camp, he found Asa, his father, and Nathan, his kinsman, sitting before the hut; and not seeing Caleb, the dog, he began to look around. Soon he discovered him stretched out at the feet of Asa. Both men got up from their seats of lambskin as they saw David appear out of the mist of the fast-coming darkness, and looked at him inquiringly.

"The peace of our Lord be with you all," the young herder said as he came to a stop before them. Asa's eyes glanced with pride at the stalwart form of his son, and he nodded gently.

"God's blessing rest upon your head," the father replied. "My heart rejoices at your return."

Then Asa turned his silver-gray head, still covered with the old felt hat, to Nathan, who had remained respectfully in the background before the reddish-gleaming fire that shed a comforting warmth around them, and gently bade him make ready the supper for David. Silently Nathan obeyed. He entered the hut a moment later with a tray upon which lay a piece of mutton and a small portion of baked rice, enticingly surrounded by a row of dates and olives. Placing the tray upon the rough surface of a large stone that served the herders as a table, Nathan took a small water jar that stood near the door and sprinkled some of its contents over the hands of his kinsman. This done, he put the jar back again into its customary place by the door and returned to his seat by the fire.

Nathan was a cousin to David on his mother's side. He was the older of the two. Orphaned in childhood, he and David had grown up together. The two young men, seen together, gave to the eye a picture of a strong contrast. David's fine, open face and well-formed body were pleasing to the eye; but one would behold almost with awe the giant form of Nathan that towered almost a head above the six-foot frame of David. His torso was supported by a pair of muscular legs. His large hands and sunburnt arms suggested the strength of a bull in the co-ordinated play of strong muscles running up to a pair of broad shoulders. But a well-proportioned hooknose, a broad, good-natured mouth, and a rock-hard bearded jaw gave the face an expression of confidence and tenderness.

Motionless the giant sat, waiting patiently for David to speak, and noticed with anxiety the nervous flicker in old Asa's eyes as he watched David finish his meal. After David had eaten, he took the plate back into the hut and, when he returned, crossed over to the side of his father. The two men looked at each other for a long moment.

"My father," the young man said, slowly bending his knees, "my heart, that overflows from the bounty of the Lord, craves a blessing from your hands for the son that was born unto me but yesterday."

The seamed and wrinkled face above him seemed to grow younger at these words, and for a while silence reigned before the little hut. For this indeed was precious news to the old herder. With eyes moist, he slowly laid his gnarled hand on the bowed head of his son and whispered softly, "A grandson! O Lord, let him bring joy and honor to Thy holy name, and let him walk ever in Thy ways before Thee."

Nathan's smile showed his feeling of gladness as he slowly rose from his seat and congratulated the young father. A thankful glance from David's eyes showed his appreciation of the good wishes of his kinsman. Then he spoke.

"Tomorrow, if the Lord will, ye shall see him," David said.

"And this we will, my son," Asa replied with enthusiasm.

After this, they sat down by the red embers of the fire, their thoughts and conversation centering around the young child. David told them about the birthmark and looked expectantly for some response from his father, who, after some hesitation, said, "Son," and the old man's voice was solemn and firm, "the time of the manifestation of the Messiah is drawing nigh."

David was puzzled at the words of his father, and he could find no ready explanation of them. Over Nathan's face passed a look of helplessness as he tried to understand what he old man meant, and he looked in bewilderment at David. But before the latter could voice his surprise, Asa startled the two men even more with his next words while looking intently at his son. "Do you know Caleb, the Idumean?" he inquired.

"Yea, my father, I know the infidel," mechanically David answered. "But why do you want to know this?"

After Asa had related to his son the affair that had taken place in the afternoon between the Idumean and the dog, he said, "And now, my son, you have the reason for my question."

David was still somewhat bewildered at his father's sudden question and hesitated for a moment to answer it. But noticing the old man's anxiety for an explanation, he decided to tell him the cause of the dog's attack on the courtier.

"This Idumean and the dog met once before," David began, "I found the fiend attempting to violate the sanctity of my home at Bethlehem. I promptly gave him the punishment he deserved. I thought he was unarmed, but, at the very moment when I turned my back to him, he came at me with a knife. He would have succeeded in his murderous intention, had it not been for the watchful eye of our faithful dog. For suddenly Caleb sank his fangs into the wrist of the coward, who then begged for mercy, which I foolishly granted him. And this, my father, is the explanation for the dog's behavior this afternoon."

Asa's face expressed satisfaction as he petted the head of the sheep dog curled at his feet, and, looking at his son, he remarked, "It will be well for us to be prepared for some mischief from the hands of this wretch."

To this word of caution Nathan groaned his assent.

Asa's Secret Dreams

ECAUSE their thoughts and minds were still filled with
the happenings of the day, sleep fled from their eyes.
Hours later they were sitting by the fire, talking. A
cool breeze, that had earlier brought comfort and
refreshment from over the gray ridge of Bethlehem, now
made the old man shiver, compelling him to move closer to
the fire, in disregard of David's well-meant advice to seek
rest and sleep.

"David, my son," Asa said, trying to explain his refusal to
sleep, "when a person is young and filled with the pulsating
vigor of life, he will not notice the passing of time, but when
the summer and autumn of life are passed, then, my son, he
wishes to stop the flight of time, and he wonders how many
years of grace will still be his portion."

Something akin to alarm was in the eyes of the two young
men as they glanced at the speaker. Never before in the
many nights they had thus sat together had they heard such
words from the man their hearts adored.

"Wonder not when I speak to you in such a way," Asa
continued, "and do not misinterpret my words. I am not
afraid of death, for I have received many blessings from the
Lord my God. Do I not possess a worthy son? And since
yesterday my heart has delighted in the thought of having
a grandson. Yes, indeed I should be a happy man, but to my
sorrow I must admit that I am not."

David, at a loss as to the meaning of his father's words,
inquired softly, "May I ask you, O father, what it is that

prevents your happiness?"

Asa, nodding his gray head, stared into the glossy darkness of the young night and said, "It is the thought of the degeneration of my people under the Roman yoke, fostered by the Idumean, that fills my breast with bitterness. When I behold the dawn of a new day and my eyes look with rapture over yonder valley, then happiness fills my soul. But Satan ruled the day when this blessing became a curse to me, for Herod built his place of abomination on yonder hill. Then the peace of this valley vanished. I am part of those hills. They were the playground of my childhood. They saw me grow to manhood, and it was to them that I told my happiness as your blessed mother bore you, a son, unto me. Those hills, too, were the silent witness of my deep sorrow, when I laid her to rest for her last sleep. I saw generations come and go. Many of them were dear to my heart. Time and change brought disappointment to countless hearts. They had all been hoping for the manifestation of the promised Redeemer and Messiah of Israel, but the silent grave claimed them ere they could realize their hopes and dreams."

An uncomfortable silence settled over the little group by the fire as the old herder ended. The latter sat with his eyes turned toward the fire, his mind still filled with the thoughts of yesterday. The two young men were loath to break the stillness that was so unusual to them.

From the direction of the road below the camp came the shouts of angry camel drivers as they pressed their animals for more haste. The noise of coming horsemen also came to their ears. From the narrow windows of the distant palace, that loomed like a large monster in the darkness, came the pin-points of yellow lights. Caleb the dog, who performed sentinel duty at the sheepfold, came limping back to lay himself at the feet of David.

At length David broke the prolonged silence and said, "You have told us of your forlorn hope, O father, for the coming of this Messiah to our people. But have you ever thought of this, that the hour of His manifestation has not yet arrived? I confess that I know a little about this hope of yours, and I pray you tell me more of it, if you will. Are there any signs that would proclaim His coming?"

A slight trace of a smile came for a moment into the deep-set eyes of Asa as he looked at his son and said, "I am no scholar who is able to tell you all that is written about Him. I know only that it is written in the book of the prophet Micah that this our beloved Bethlehem should be the birthplace of the Anointed One. To your inquiry if there would be a sign, I cannot answer you. For I know not of the existence of such a one. But I am fully convinced that when the time of His revelation is at hand, a sign will herald His birth."

David, listening to his father's words, had not the slightest idea of the high thoughts that slumbered behind the wrinkled forehead of the old man. Asa was thinking of his grandson and the star on the infant's back. "Could not this star be the sign indicating him as the Messiah? For does not many a young Jewish mother hope to bear the Messiah? Why could it not be his grandson?"

The thought of this possibility drove the herder from his seat, and he walked away from the fire, which Nathan had kept going by feeding it occasionally with pieces of camel dung.

The eyes of the two young men followed Asa as he slowly walked over to the sheepfold, with the limping Caleb behind him.

"Your father's heart is troubled," Nathan remarked to the brooding David, "and his thoughts are disturbed in his ardent desire to witness the manifestation of the promised Redeemer of our people. He so greatly desires it that he even dares to think of his grandson as the Messiah."

David considered for a while the words of his friend and then replied, "Your words are the echo of my own heart, O Nathan, and I feel distressed at not being able to console my father. He and I and you also, as you know, are of the house of Benjamin, and not from the line of King David, from which some day will come the Messiah. My father is not ignorant of this, but his old heart is tired and is subject to strange notions. So let us comfort him as best we can, for his days of hope are indeed numbered."

VII

The Glorious Message

A LITTLE while later Asa came back from his visit to the fold where he had gone to look after his sheep, and nothing in his face betrayed the turmoil in his soul as he said, "Let us go seek the comfort of sleep, for tomorrow I shall see my grandson."

Suddenly the three men were mystified by the loud bark of the dog. Wonderingly they began to look around, but could find no cause for the dog's alarm. Caleb refused to be quieted and began to whimper. Suddenly tucking his tail down between his legs, he rushed to the entrance of the hut as if to seek shelter and protection from some impending danger. Their curiosity became more pronounced as they began to scan the darkness above them. The next moment they looked at one another, their eyes filled with perplexity.

The velvet darkness of the heavens seemed to retreat before the advance of an eerie light, whose intensity was lessened for a time by a dense fog which enveloped the entire region about them. The hills and the valley and all nature around them seemed to stop breathing as if awaiting a word from the Creator. The sheep, too, were acting strangely. A moment before, they had lain on the dew-covered ground, chewing their cud in contentment and peace. Now they could be seen huddled together into a flock of terror-stricken creatures. But the herders gave all this only a fleeting glance, for their eyes were fixed on the sky. Not a star could be seen. The crescent moon was the only visible feature in the great wide dome of heaven.

How long they had stood in awed wonder none of them remembered later. All at once the heavy fog seemed to lift, as if rolled back by an unseen hand, revealing to their startled eyes a picture of celestial grandeur. And a brightness, many times greater than the brightness of the sun at noonday, shone all around and began to envelop them. The herders seemed rooted to the ground. Nathan, inclined to superstition, started to flee, but his limbs would not obey his will. And as he cast a hasty glance at his companions, he became still more confused, for they too were sore amazed and in terror were hiding their faces in the palms of their hands, as if to shut out the awesome vision. Asa trembled as if ravaged by a fever.

Now a strange sound, something akin to music, reached their ears. Amid this heavenly glory, which surpassed all else that had ever occurred up to this time, appeared the form of an angel clothed in a snow-white garment. Terrorstricken, the three men fell to the ground, convinced in their hearts that the day of judgment had arrived. But soon a voice from the heavens brought calm and reassurance to their troubled minds: "Fear not, for, behold, I bring you good tidings of great joy, which shall be to all people. For unto you is born this day in the city of David a Savior, which is Christ the Lord."

Asa lifted his eyes, that now reflected a new hope, and whispered, "A Savior!" And like an echo of the words the angel had spoken came the words from his quivering lips, "And as a sign unto you, you shall find the Babe wrapped in swaddling clothes, lying in a manger."

The sound of music and singing began to grow in volume, and the song, "Glory to God in the highest, and on earth peace, good will to men!" filled with rapture the hearts of the three men as they beheld the multitude of heavenly singers slowly disappearing into the misty clouds of the night.

Fear no longer held the herders, and a quiet peace settled upon them. And as their eyes became again accustomed to the returning darkness, they looked at one another for a long while, each hesitating to express in words the thought and feeling that filled his mind and soul. The two young herders watched the old man as he stood still gazing into the sky. His lips were moving as if in prayer. And when he turned to his son and kinsman, he revealed a face transfigured with joy.

"David, my son," he whispered, "was this a dream, or have I heard aright that the Savior has come?" His voice broke as he stood with folded hands, giving expression to the joy that possessed him, and said, "The great Jehovah has heard my prayer. He has sent us His Redeemer and has granted me the privilege of beholding Him with these mortal eyes of mine."

All fatigue forgotten, the old man stopped before the entrance of the hut and resolutely declared, "I shall not lay me down to sleep until I have seen the Savior."

As if in response to the declaration of the old herder, David quietly entered the hut for a moment and returned with the staff and an old coat of sheepskin for his father to use against the growing chill of the advancing night. Leaving the care of the sheep to the faithful dog Caleb, Asa and his two companions left for Bethlehem.

VIII

No Room in the Inn

THE three men hurried in silence along the old caravan road, which now seemed deserted. Asa went ahead despite his age. And it was not until the shadowy outline of the town came into view that he walked more slowly and turned to David and Nathan, and asked, "Where shall we look for the Babe?"

David eyed his father for a moment, seeing the point of his inquiry, and replied quickly, "Fear not, O father, I know where to find the child. There is only one place where it could be found, and that is at the khan. You remember the words of the angel, 'Ye shall find the Babe lying in a manger.' And where else," David added, "could we find a manger except at the khan?"

Asa and Nathan acknowledged the truth in David's words, and followed him silently as they continued their journey. With increasing vigor they began to climb the terraced hill to the summit, passing through the moon-lit gardens of the town. Passing the ancient Well of David, they came to a stop before a structure a single story high. This was the khan (better known as the village inn). A lighted lantern, which hung suspended from a wooden beam above the entrance, threw its feeble rays into the night. The inn, built of rough stones, consisted of a square enclosure for the housing of cattle. Along the walls were the leewans (little rooms), built a foot or so above the level of the courtyard for the accommodation of travelers. These leewans were small and low, without a front wall, the interior of each open to the gaze of anyone who happened to be near.

The three men stood hesitant for a moment, looking at a powerful, gray-bearded man who at the moment had stepped over the threshold of the paneled gate. He was the keeper of the inn. Moving toward them with a cautious, measured step, he inquired in a deep voice, "Ho there! And what may be your desire in this locality at this hour of the night? There is no room for the likes of you, so be gone!"

But when the herders approached closer to him, he exclaimed in astonishment, "Of all the surprises, if it isn't my old friend Asa!" Grasping the willing hand of the old herder and pressing it vigorously, he tried to offer an excuse for his former harsh words, and then in a more cordial manner he asked, "What, my friend, brings you hither at such a late hour?"

Asa did not reply for a moment, and as the innkeeper looked into the herder's flushed face, he felt that something of unusual importance had brought him to the khan. Asa's words confirmed this feeling when he said, "Reuben, my friend, where is the newborn King of our people, for He is born this very night?"

The aged innkeeper moved a little closer to the herder, laying a gnarled hand on the latter's shoulder, and said with a trace of pity in his voice, "Are you ill, my friend, or has age addled your brain? I know of no newborn King of our people."

His gaze lingered on young David for a moment as if to seek an explanation from him concerning his father's behavior. The young man understood and quickly answered for his father. "No, good Reuben, my father has not lost his reason, and if you would know, it was the joy in his heart that caused him to ask you this question. We have come to find the Savior as it was made known to us by the angel of the Lord."

Then David explained the whole matter to the innkeeper, and when he noticed the look of doubt on the old man's face, he said, "You do not believe me, and for this I blame you not. But I have spoken the truth. The Savior has been born, and if you know where we can find Him, tell us, that we need tarry here no longer."

The innkeeper was amazed at the words he had just heard and looked at the three herders for a long time, trying to grasp the meaning of it all. Finally, after some thought, he said, "It seems strange indeed that you three men could have had the same dream at one and the same time. There must be some truth in what you have told me. But you will not find this newborn King here. For I know of none, unless it be the little son of Joseph of Nazareth and his young wife Mary. He was born in my stable about midnight. But no royal cradle awaited the little Babe, for His mother, in want of one, was obliged to lay Him in a manger."

Asa had listened with intense interest to the conversation of his son and the innkeeper, and had become somewhat impatient. But when he heard Reuben's last words, he shouted for joy, "It is He! O friend, please lead us to this Babe!"

Reuben nodded with excusable doubt and, turning away from them, said: "Tarry ye here. I will return quickly."

They saw him disappear through the gate of the inn and return a moment later carrying a lighted lantern in his right hand. He motioned his friends to follow him. As he led the way past the inn, they entered a narrow ravine a few hundred feet distant from the khan. A short while later, the old innkeeper halted momentarily, and the herders saw before them the dark mouth of a cave. The distinct odor of cattle and hay touched their nostrils. Reuben stopped before the latticed door, pushed it slowly inward, and with his silent companions entered a narrow passage not more than five feet wide. A short distance farther on they saw a large room poorly lighted by a tallow torch stuck in a crevice near the entrance. To their right were a few head of cattle, tied to a manger with pieces of hempen rope. Most of them had bedded down and were chewing their cud in contentment.

The herders, however, took but little interest in these. It was the two persons at their left on whom they fixed their attention. Asa, filled with an urgent desire to see the King, stopped at Reuben's side as the latter addressed the gray-haired man who had risen from a bundle of wheat straw upon which he had been resting.

"The peace of the Lord be with you, O Joseph. I pray you to forgive this untimely intrusion. I have no other excuse for my action than the story which my friend Asa will impart to you." Having spoken, he introduced Asa to the carpenter of Nazareth.

A questioning glance from the eyes of the Galilean held the trembling herder. "What is it, my friend? Speak on. In what can I be of service to you?" he asked gently.

"Show me your Son, for He is the newborn King of our people. Yea, He is more than that: He is the Savior, the long-awaited Messiah of Israel," Asa answered jubilantly.

Before the speechless Joseph could answer, Asa had moved away from him. He knelt beside the manger, that ran along the base of the wall, and lifted his folded hands in adoration as his old eyes came to rest on the face of the tiny Infant in swaddling clothes lying in peaceful slumber in the depth of the manger. "My cup of happiness and joy runneth over, O Lord, for I am permitted to behold the Redeemer of my people," he whispered. The softly whispered words of joy sank deep into the tender heart of the young mother, who reposed in a deep bed of soft straw made for her beside the manger.

David and Nathan looked with adoration at the young mother's angelic face, which reflected a wondrous beauty as her tender eyes rested on her sleeping son and the worshiping Asa. After the first wave of joy had subsided somewhat, the herders told their glorious story. Now a heavenly peace filled the heart of Joseph, for his dream, confirmed by the story of the herders, that his little Son was conceived by the Holy Ghost, was reality indeed.

David and Nathan turned to gaze once more at the happy mother before they departed. "By what name, O Mary, will this your Son be known?" David asked her.

"He shall be called Jesus," she smiled up to him and added softly, "for He shall save His people from their sins."

If the young herder was puzzled by her words, he showed no signs of it, and with delight he told her of his own son so recently born to him by his wife Elizabeth.

Gray dawn broke over the summit of Bethlehem as the herders left the inn. Asa, still filled with joy, eagerly told the glorious news to all who cared to listen. And it was in this way that Melchor, a stable boy from the palace, received the information about the newborn King of the Jews. If old Asa could have looked into the future at this moment, his heart would have been heavy with sorrow. But he did not know of the dark clouds gathering around him and his loved ones because of his readiness to spread the glad tidings.

IX

David at the Temple

THE days that followed the birth of Christ were days of cloudless joy for Asa and his family, and this joy reached its height whenever he looked at his grandson. He was pleased too at the choice of the name "Jonathan" which the parents had given to their son. "For he will be the sunshine of mine old days, a precious gift from the Lord," he would often say to himself.

Returning a few days later to the khan, Asa, to his sorrow, found that Joseph had departed from the cave with his family. The old gatekeeper could give him but little information as to their whereabouts. Asa left the inn with a feeling of disappointment.

Meanwhile David and Elizabeth were busy preparing themselves for their trip to Jerusalem, the latter to present herself and her son for purification at the Temple. Over his right shoulder David carried a yearling lamb, pure white, without blemish, intended as a burnt offering. And on the tender breast of the young mother nestled a turtle dove, intended as the sin offering. David, with the payment of five shekels (the equivalent of three dollars) bought Jonathan's freedom from Temple service, which the law would otherwise have required of him.

As they were leaving the colonnaded porch of Solomon, they were pleasantly surprised to see the carpenter from Nazareth and Mary, his young wife, with the little Babe in her arms. The latter was the attraction for many eyes as the little family stood before a tall, aged man. Slowly drawing nearer to the group, David recognized this man as one called Simeon, a just and devout Israelite, esteemed and respected by many throughout Judea. His feeble hands were holding the Babe of the Manger, his eyes reflecting the joy which he now began to express with trembling lips. "Lord, now lettest Thou thy servant depart in peace, for mine eyes have seen Thy salvation, which Thou hast prepared before the face of all people. A light to lighten the Gentiles, and the glory of Thy people of Israel."

David listened to the words with understanding and was proud of not having to share the ignorance of many others who knew not their meaning. But hearing the last few words of the patriarch, something akin to anger quickened David's pulse. "A curse on the Gentiles," he said, "this King shall be only for the glory of Israel."

Broodingly David, his mind filled with disturbing thoughts, left the Temple. He, the simple man from the hills, was puzzled. He did not then realize that Simeon's words pointed to the redemption of all mankind.

A few days after their return from Jerusalem, Elizabeth became ill and was confined to her bed, thus making it necessary for David to remain at home.

One evening a week later, Marcus, the Centurion, stopped at the gate of the little garden, which fronted the small cottage, and looked for some sign from within. David's face lit up when he beheld the Roman, and, rushing to the door, he waited for Marcus as the latter came slowly up the garden path.

"This is indeed a pleasant surprise, O Marcus. You honor us with a visit," David said, bowing.

Together the two friends entered the spacious front room, where David thus excused himself, "Please be seated, and I will tell Elizabeth of your arrival."

The soldier nodded smilingly and removed his polished helmet and placed it upon the sanded top of the table which served David and his small family not only as a dining table but also as a gathering place when matters of importance were to be decided. Stretching out his long limbs before him, and leaning back his head so that it came to rest against the wall, the centurion's mind went back a number of years when he first met David and his father. And whenever he thought of them, the bond of friendship between him and the two seemed to grow stronger. He still could remember the time when he had come out of his stupor and delirium, as he lay on a lambskin-covered cot in the hut at Asa's sheep camp. At the time he had no idea as to the cause of his being there. But his aching body, covered with many wounds, caused him to recall the ambush into which he had fallen a few hours before; and to recall how old Asa, who hovered about him, had encouraged him with his soft but steady voice, and with gentle hands had assuaged the pain in his aching body. He would often call to mind the words of his old friend, "You are a very sick person, O Roman, and if it had not been for the guiding hand of the Lord, you would now be a dead man."

As it happened, after he had fought a losing battle with a band of fanatical Zealots, extremists of the national party, who had ambushed him as he was coming along the road from Jericho, David and Nathan, by putting the attackers to flight, arrived just in time to save the Roman from certain death. Knowing that without immediate help he could not live, they brought him to Asa's camp. From this time on a beautiful friendship had continued between the three herders and himself.

His thoughts were interrupted as David came back into the room, closely followed by his wife, who held little Jonathan in her arms. David's face shone with pride as the blushing mother pushed aside the thin veil of gauze and exposed the features and the small but tightly clenched fist of the infant. Marcus, bending over the boy, smiled at Elizabeth and playfully caressed one of the little fists with his finger. The little fellow awakened at the touch and looked at him. His little fist opened, and the tiny fingers closed around the finger of the soldier.

The heart of the Centurion was moved. The expression of his eyes told his friends of the secret sorrow of his life. Leonia his wife was childless. As if to shake off the distressing thought, Marcus smiled at the two happy people and with a tinge of irony said, "It is a pity that the little fellow must become a sheepherder, and not a soldier as I had hoped."

To this David replied with a slight tone of resentment in his voice, "My friend, a poor sheepherder once became a mighty warrior and king. But one has never heard that a soldier could become a good sheepherder!"

Marcus felt the barb and smiled apologetically at his friend. "That is right. I deserve the rebuke. But I meant no offense. Pray forgive me my thoughtless words," he replied.

Elizabeth, reading the inmost thoughts of the soldier, answered for her husband. "There is nothing to forgive, O Roman. For one cannot always control the desires of the heart. Have faith and continue to hope, and perhaps a son will yet be given to you."

The woman did not realize that her words, uttered out of pity, were really prophetic.

One hour later, the centurion left, accompanied by David a short distance along the road. In the course of their conversation David happened to think of Caleb the Herodian, and related to his friend the incident between Asa and the captain. "And I fear the evil mind of the courtier has not forgotten it," David ended.

"In this, my friend, you do well not to underestimate the cunning of the knave, for I happen to know him. Watch out for him. He will strike when you are least prepared and the odds are all on his side. If ever you are in need of help, call on me," Marcus said seriously.

Warm and sincere were the warning words of the Roman as he took leave of his friend David.

X

Master and Servant

CAPTAIN CALEB, of the household guard of Herod, rode as one possessed of a demon as he left old Asa standing in the road. His pride, his vanity, was hurt to such an extent that it boded no good to those who had given offense to him. The sting of the insult to his person made him plunge the long-spiked spurs deep into the flanks of the horse, which squealed in pain at the inhuman treatment. Caleb's hatred grew still deeper as he remembered the humiliation he had suffered at the hands of David. "By the beard of my father," he cursed under his breath, "I shall make them pay dearly for this!"

The battlement of the palace loomed before him in the last golden rays of the sun. The sentry on guard, recognizing the approaching horseman, hastened to throw open wide the mighty wings of the gate. The captain, ignoring the respectful salute of the sentry, cast his haughty eyes about as he rode through the gate into the spacious courtyard. Pulling his sweating horse to an abrupt halt at the base of a beautiful stairway that was crowned with a colonnade of reddish marble, marking the entrance to his apartment, he leaped from the saddle. Looking for a moment around him, he began to grip the stock of the lead-loaded horsewhip as his baleful eyes watched the figure of a stable boy who came running toward him from the interior of the horse stable.

"Miserable wretch!" the captain thundered, "is this the way to serve your master? This perhaps will teach you to be at hand the next time I arrive!" and lifting his arm, he lashed the whip with force into the face of the fear-stricken boy. Covering the bloody welt with trembling hands, the lad cowered on his knees before his tormentor, who watched from slitted eyes for a sign of resistance or protest from the menial. But none came. Then silently the mistreated servant took hold of the reins which hung from the foam-covered mouth of the animal and led the horse toward the stable.

Jesup, a dark-complexioned young man, about twenty years of age, dressed in the livery of a palace servant, hastily set down a cup of wine from which he was about to drink as Caleb entered the apartment. The captain roared in haughty laughter as he noticed the expression of guilt and confusion in the features of the valet, and remarked with deceiving mirth, "I see you find it quite in order to help yourself to a drink from your master's wine!" And glancing at the golden cup, he continued, "And it gives you no scruples to employ this cup of mine!"

The valet's face was filled with fear as he retreated from the malicious smile of the captain, and, as if in acknowledgment of his guilt, he fell to his knees. Yet no plea for pity or mercy escaped his trembling lips. The beady eyes of the soldier as he scowled at his servant expressed his pride in his power to command. Playing menacingly with the horse-whip in his hands, Caleb exclaimed, "Get up! For this time I shall spare you the punishment you so greatly deserve." Dropping the whip on the floor, he threw himself wearily upon the comfortable cushions of a couch and demanded a cup of wine. "But be you careful, my servant," he taunted, "that you do not use the cup which your lips have defiled, or," throwing an ominous glance at the whip on the floor, "I shall repent of the mercy just now shown you."

Jesup hastened to comply with the wish of the captain and handed him the drink. As the valet was retreating respectfully toward the door, the captain's sharp order brought him to a sudden stop. After bidding him approach nearer, the captain said invitingly, "Come here, my friend. Go help yourself to the drink of which my unexpected arrival has robbed you. I will give you the cup as a remembrance of my good will toward you."

Dumbfounded by the abrupt change of tone, the servant did as he was bidden. The questioning stare of his eyes reflected his perplexity. The young lad could not understand the seeming generosity of the captain, and his thoughts flew back to the days when the slightest mistake had brought him severe punishment. Many a time he had rued the hour when he entered the service of the Herodian. But, born of poor parents, he had become possessed of the ambition to become sufficiently prosperous to repay his people for the years of privation and poverty which they had undergone in providing for his earlier guidance and training. In the hope of reaching this goal quickly, he had entered the palace service as valet to the favorite of Herod. But to his great sorrow, instead of the dreamed-of wealth, he had reaped abuse and sometimes cruel whippings. He had tried to leave the service of the Idumean, but to no avail. The captain was not a man to set at liberty a servant who knew many of his dark deeds and secrets.

Jesup was a handsome lad. The livery he wore, in colors of red and blue, covered a small but perfectly knit body. A pair of soft, brown eyes with black eyelashes gave his face the expression of a dreamer. And the well-shaped nose, above a tender-lipped mouth, together with the long jaw of a Syrian, denoted a character moved and ruled by emotion. Black hair, carefully kept, hung in ringlets to the base of his well-formed neck.

Handing the empty cup back to the valet, Caleb began to

stretch his long legs with a satisfied grunt, and said with a hidden glance into the face of Jesup, "Now let us have the news, if there is any."

Jesup, hearing the question, thought he had found the answer to his master's generosity of the moment before. Caleb wanted to be informed of the latest news and gossip of the palace since his departure a week before. Jesup hesitated for a moment as he looked into the face of his master, who was becoming irritated at the valet's apparent hesitancy, but soon replied, "My lord, your presence is required at his majesty's chambers as soon after your return as possible." And the voice of Jesup fell to a whisper, when he said, "If I might be so bold, I would like to give you warning that he is in a bad and desperate mood."

The captain's eyes opened a little wider as he studied the words of his servant. Anxiety and a trace of fear swept over him. Rising to a sitting position, he closed his deep-set eyes as if to hide the turbulent thoughts that were at work behind the low forehead. Then he asked, "And do you, my good Jesup, know the reason that might have caused this desperate mood of my sovereign?"

"That I do, my lord," the valet hastily replied. "And it is not a secret to anyone in the palace. Prince Antipater is in the dungeon, condemned to die."

The captain's features turned ashen as he jumped up suddenly from the couch, and, digging his talonlike fingers into the shoulders of his servant, he cried sharply, "Knave, you lie, for I know the prince to be in Rome and far away from the unhealthy atmosphere that follows his footsteps in the court of his royal father!"

A slight noise from the door caused him to stop suddenly and to turn toward the suave face of Limus, the personal valet of the king, who had just entered the apartment. After receiving permission to speak, the valet said, "My royal master desires to have speech with thee, my lord."

Suppressing with great effort the storm that had risen anew within him, the captain, with a malicious grin lurking at the corners of his thin-lipped mouth, nodded haughtily to the king's messenger as the latter left the room.

"I wonder if he heard what was said," the captain murmured under his breath, as he turned to the motionless form of his servant. "How many days," he inquired of Jesup, "has the noble prince been in the dungeon? And how in heaven's name did he ever get there?" Caleb, the proud and ruthless despot, was indeed worried as he listened nervously to every word of his servant's reply.

"It was the day after your departure for Jericho," Jesup said, "that the prince arrived at the palace in the custody of a strong guard of Thracians. After a short interview with his royal father, I saw him marched off to the dungeon where he now is. And if thou wilt permit me, my lord, to speak freely, I am afraid that his days of grace are numbered, because of Salome, the king's sister. She arrived from Caesarea only yesterday, and she was immediately called into her brother's presence as soon as the king was advised of her arrival."

"Hm! That is why I was sent on a fool's errand," the captain exploded in disgust, turning away. "I fear me no good of this, and I shall watch my every step."

XI

Herod, Called the Great

NIGHT had now fallen. But despite the refreshing coolness that filled the mighty corridor and hall, into which he had entered, Caleb felt the blood rush hot through his veins at the thought of what might be ahead of him. He knew that he was in a dangerous position and, if found out, he would share the lot of Antipater. His uneasiness grew, and his roving eye marked the increased number of guards placed at every door leading into the king's apartments. Paying scant attention to the respectful salutes of the guards, he went to the end of the long corridor and through a small door entered the antechamber of the king. The shadowy form of Limus detached itself from the narrow frame of a window and confronted him.

"Permit me, my lord," he said, "and I will announce your arrival to my gracious master." And as the captain tried to pass by him, the valet's commanding "Halt!" arrested his step and stopped the haughty words that were forming in his mind. "No one, my noble captain," Limus continued, "will enter the bedchamber of my king unless he has my approval. Explicit orders from my sovereign."

Caleb was thunderstruck at the unexpected action of the Greek, but offered little protest as he was being relieved of the dagger in his girdle. "My master also gave orders prohibiting the carrying of weapons in his presence," coolly remarked the valet.

Limus, hiding the weapon in the folds of his own garment,

left the bewildered courtier and disappeared through a door into the bedchamber of Herod. A few moments later he reappeared and ushered the frightened soldier over the threshold to face the king.

The furnishings of the large room told of the love of its owner for luxury and beauty. The bright illumination from six large candelabra fastened in brackets to the ceiling and walls was reflected in a soft mellow tone from the four golden bedposts, each of which was ornamented with a lion's head finial. Four large windows, their frames filled with beautiful stained glass, permitted a view of the valley, where fertile fields nestled close to the castle hill. Heavy, artistically patterned rugs covered the floor, and some could be seen hanging on the walls of red marble, softening the otherwise austere atmosphere that pervaded the room. Two braziers, resting on tops of marble blocks two feet high near the door, were filled with heavily scented burning charcoal, watched and fed by a little Nubian slave. The bed itself stood in the narrow confines of an alcove, affording its royal occupant a clear view of the entire room. On the wall above the head of the bed could be seen a vast array of weapons. Slender-shafted jereeds, the favorite lances of the Arabs, vied in grace and beauty with ivory-hilted daggers and swords forged by master hands at Damascus.

As the trembling captain beheld the reclining form of the king wrapped in a blanket of costly furs, his mind reverted for a moment to the days when this wreck of a man had been a handsome picture of perfect manhood. The swarthy complexion of the face and skin told of his origin. He was more Arab than Jew. The hawklike nose and pointed black beard revealed a forceful character. That was the Herod the captain remembered.

But all that was left of him now was the indomitable will

and cunning which thirty and some odd years before had put him on the throne of ancient Judea. He was a descendant of one Antipater, governor of Idumea. By birth an Arab, this Antipater became a Jew to further his political ambition. Through extraordinary and valuable service to the great Julius Caesar, he was made procurator under Hyrcanus, hereditary high priest of Judea. He had two sons, Phasaelus the elder, and Herod the younger.

Herod, grown to manhood and put in charge of Galilee, began to crush into the dust everyone who dared resist him in his rise to power. After his father had become the victim of an assassin, the old high priest came wholly under the evil influence of Herod. The murderer of his father was apprehended and put to death by torture, through connivance of Herod and against the will of the royal Hyrcanus.

Provoked by his enterprises and insults against the Sanhedrin, a number of wealthy and prominent Jews made accusations against him to the mighty Antony, who at that time held sway over Judea in the name of Caesar. But the cunning brain of Herod and a large bribe gained not only vindication for himself, but brought him a great deal nearer the goal of his ambition. He was made tetrarch with full political powers, which fact made Hyrcanus a person of little importance. A few years later, during which time he was subject to ever-changing situations, he became king of Judea by the order of the great Augustus. But his position as king was in no wise secure, for the loyalty of the people still clung to Hyrcanus of the royal house of the Asmoneans. Not even the union with Mariamne, who became his wife, and who was the granddaughter of Hyrcanus, could dispel the dislike of the people toward him. They were well aware of his origin and treated him as a schemer as well as a foreigner. Cruelty and force marked his reign henceforth.

Mariamne bore him two sons, Alexander and Aristobulus. Herod really loved Mariamne. She was the only person who had ever held sway over his heart. The two princes were sent to Rome, where they came under the influence of the imperial court.

Herod's sister Salome, a woman of intrigue, never liked her sister-in-law. She hated Mariamne for her noble and decided character. Cunningly feeding the jealousy of her brother, she at last succeeded in bringing about the destruction of the beautiful woman by accusing her of treason and infidelity. To all appearances, Herod gave her a fair trial, but the trial was only a matter of form, and he ordered his wife to be put to death. After her death, his love for her seemed to have returned, and his unceasing regret for his act drove him to the brink of insanity. To still the pangs of remorse, he began to satisfy his lust for blood by slaughtering hundreds of his imprisoned victims who in any way had aroused his ill will and displeasure.

Later he married many times. In the end he became a maniac. No subject of his felt secure in his presence. He filled his nights with roaring and bitter wailing when the ghosts of his countless victims drove his black soul to despair.

The two sons of Mariamne, called back from Rome, sought to avenge their mother's death, but they were frustrated in the attempt. Both were tried and sentenced to death, then strangled at Sebaste.

As Herod grew old and feeble, he looked around for a successor to his throne. He chose Antipater, his oldest son, who was living in semi-banishment in Galilee, not knowing that this Antipater had been the real cause of bringing about the death of the two sons of Mariamne. And Antipater, fearing discovery of the fact, thought it wise to get permission from the half-mad despot to pay a visit to Caesar and his court at Rome, and thus remove himself from possible harm.

Caleb, seeing himself without a position after Herod's death, had worked himself into the confidence of the future ruler and had kept the wily prince informed of everything that went on at the court of his father. But the two had underestimated the power of Salome, the king's sister. Waiting her opportunity to get her brother's ear, she poisoned his mind, telling him of the part which his successor to the throne had played in the destruction of Alexander and Aristobulus.

It was indeed a blow to the heart of the tyrant, for he had loved the sons of Mariamne with all the love he had once shown for their murdered mother and all the love of which his selfish heart was capable. Distance could not save Antipater from the wrath of the brooding and disappointed king. Under some pretext he was recalled from Rome and put into custody as soon as he landed at Caesarea.

XII

Herod and Caleb

THE captain remained motionless for many minutes, waiting for the king to speak. The dark and baleful stare of the sovereign was centered on the blanching features of his hireling, a malicious smile hanging at the corners of his drooling mouth. He had been drinking and was now idly fingering the golden cup.

At the head of the bed stood Limus the Greek, his watchful eyes filled with triumph. His mocking grin served as a warning to the captain and caused him to tremble with fear. The king, noticing this, raised his eyebrows as if in surprise.

"Why are you trembling, O captain? Are you ill?" in an assumed tone of sympathy came the words from the king. Then turning toward the valet, he said, "Perhaps a cup of wine would do him good!" And as if he had been waiting for this occasion, Limus hastened to comply with the king's desire by filling a small cup to the brim and handing it to the captain.

Caleb knew only too well that death was in that cup. He recognized the pitcher from which Limus had poured the wine as "The Pitcher of Death." Not daring to refuse the drink, he looked imploringly at Herod and, falling to his knees, stammered hoarsely, "O gracious King, spare me this cup!"

A satanic laugh from the ruler's lips made him shudder, bringing a clammy sweat to his forehead.

"Our good captain seems not to be thirsty," the king grinned over his shoulder to the watching valet. "He dares to slight the good will of his king. And why, may I ask?"

The mocking grin disappeared and was replaced by a baleful smile. And turning to the shaking captain, he cried, "I will tell you the reason why. It is the bad conscience you have for plotting against the welfare of your king. You have failed in the test of loyalty to your king and have proved to me that you are guilty of the charge of treason, and that you deserve—death!"

The captain was now on the verge of collapse and sought desperately for a lifesaving answer. Extreme fear began to grip him and to take from him for the moment the power to think. He felt that death was hovering over him. But he was not certain as to just how much the king knew of the conspiracy and what part he had played in it. The thought came to him, at the last moment, to ask what charge the king had against him, with the hope of finding a way out of the horrifying situation.

"My lord, I have served thee faithfully, and know not why the sun of thy noble countenance has turned from me, and what has caused thy anger and ill will," he said with trembling voice.

Herod, startled for a moment by the reply, looked for a second at Limus as if to ask his advice, then said darkly, "Think not, my friend, that you can lie yourself out of this. For your accuser is none other than Salome, my royal sister. She accuses you and my eldest son, Prince Antipater, of conspiring against your king. And both of you are accused by her of bringing about the death of my beloved sons Alexander and Aristobulus, whom I sent innocent to their death. Yes, innocent, you miserable wretch!"

As he mentioned the names of his sons, whom his own insane cruelty had put to death, a terrible change came over the disease-wracked features of the ruler. His eyes became bloodshot as his guilty heart tried to shut out the torturing pangs of regret, and a slimy froth drooled from his lips as he fell in convulsions into the waiting arms of his valet.

From the captain came a sigh of relief, and as he looked at the suffering king, he hoped that death would soon overtake him. Limus, who had not missed the calculating glance of the courtier, motioned to him to leave the room, with a final warning, "Take heed and let no thoughts of flight enter your mind, for my master's arm is long and will reach you wherever you might be!"

Outwardly accepting the veiled threat, Caleb swore in his heart to destroy the wily Greek as soon as Antipater should come to the throne. And with a last, deep bow toward the bed, upon which tossed the groaning form of the king, the captain left the room to return to his own quarters.

More Trouble for Caleb

ALMOST a whole month had passed by since the eventful hour at the apartment of the king, and Caleb felt as though he were living on borrowed time. The suspense was driving him mad.

"Why was I not called before the king again? Has the king's condition taken a turn for the worse? Or was the crafty, cunning brain of Limus behind it all?" he asked himself.

He had no way of finding the answers to these questions, for his every step was watched. He had even refused to obey the prince's call to visit him in the dungeon, for he feared a trap.

One evening, on the way to his apartment, he met Limus coming from the royal suite, and gathered sufficient courage to inquire about the king's health. An uncomfortable feeling at once took possession of him as the valet fixed his penetrating eyes on him for a long moment before he spoke. "Fear not, my lord," Limus said, "the Lion of Judea is very much alive, and he still will be able to settle your account." And with a devilish grin the Greek went past him, leaving him standing in the corridor.

The captain's daggerlike glance followed the form of Limus with such burning hatred that it brought a groan of pain to his lips. "Accursed Greek, you had better watch out or I will find ways and means to settle your account first!" he swore under his breath.

Storming out from the semidark hall, he descended the

broad steps of the marble stairway into the courtyard, his gimlet eyes seeking an outlet for the fury that raged within him. And soon they came to rest on a small group of people by the main gate. Three beautiful white dromedaries were kneeling before the entrance to the guardhouse, their riders just then dismounting. Wondering, he hastened closer, pushing his way through a ring of curious soldiers and menials from the palace, and confronted the strangers. "What is the meaning of this?" Arrogantly and impatiently came the question, as he faced the sergeant of the guardhouse. Over the battle-scarred features of the officer rose an amused grin as he slowly replied, "These three gentlemen have come seeking the newborn King of the Jews."

Caleb, aware of his waning prestige and power at the palace, tried not to notice the joke of the old soldier—for that is what he thought it was—and turned about to face the strangers. His eyes noticed with envy the beautifully tooled saddle-gear and trappings of the regal animals, and a calculating look masked his eyes as he thus addressed the three riders, "What is it you desire, my good sirs? What seek ye here?"

One of the three, with a face of perfect Grecian form, looked mildly at him with a pair of clear, blue eyes and replied with a deep, rich voice, "We have come to seek the newborn King of the Jews."

If the ground before him had opened suddenly, he could not have been more shocked than he was as he listened to the man. "What is the meaning of all this?" he began to ask himself. "First the sergeant, now the stranger." Noticing again the amused grin of his subaltern, he spat angrily. "If this is a joke at my expense, I will make you pay dearly for it!" he exclaimed.

But when Melchior the Greek explained the object of the quest, Caleb's mind became filled with confusion and worry.

Noticing the curious eyes of the crowd, he decided to invite the three old men to his own apartment. He wished to ask them more about the matter before permitting them to see the king. At the apartment Jesup was ordered to serve refreshments, while the captain continued in conversation with the three men.

"Where and how, my honored sirs, did you hear about this newborn King?" he asked them finally. "Indeed I can give you no information about him. I know of no king except my lord Herod, the Lion of Judea."

"Well spoken, most honored captain," the Greek replied softly. "We all understand your justified doubts about the existence of this King, whom we seek, and honor your loyalty to Herod the Great. But if you must know, we are astrologers. Studying the stars is our profession. From them we have received the knowledge that we are privileged to pay our homage to this newborn King of the Jews."

Caleb sighed with relief, hearing this, and came to the conclusion that the whole thing must be a hoax, some strange idea of the warped brains of the strangers.

"Where," he asked with a smile, "does this supposed King hold court, and where does he abide?"

"This, my worthy captain," Balthasar, the dark-complexioned Egyptian, replied, "we do not know as yet, but we have seen His star, which has led us hither thus far."

Standing undecided, without speaking, Caleb turned away and left the room to seek an audience with the king.

Herod, still weak from his latest sickness, looked at his former favorite with marked suspicion, as Limus ushered him into the bedchamber. The valet, stepping to the bedside, began to whisper for a moment to the irritable ruler, who after a while nodded knowingly to his servant and cast a quick glance at the humble form of his captain, who was standing by the door.

The valet left and soon returned with the three strangers, who, bowing deeply by the bedside of the king, related their story.

Caleb trembled with fear as he listened to the words of the strangers, and his eyes did not leave the face of his master, as he noticed the turbulent emotion in the royal countenance which seemed to demand from him an immediate explanation of the matter. Though this display of emotion lasted for only a moment, the captain was convinced that uncomfortable hours were ahead.

Herod suppressed the impulse to rant, for, with hatred in his heart, it was torture for him to listen to the words the Magi had spoken. But with his iron will he managed to force a kind of smile as he again turned to his visitors. Reclining on the cushions of his bed, as if wearied and exhausted, he bade them remain as his honored guests until he should be able to give them a satisfactory answer.

As soon as the three men had left the chamber with Limus the valet, Herod called the frightened captain to his side and ordered him to bring into his presence the scribes and sages of the Sanhedrin, who were well versed in rabbinic lore.

Happy in the thought that the ruler's mind was now distracted by matters which did not endanger his personal safety, Caleb hastened to dispatch speedy messengers to the members of the Jewish tribunal, advising them of the king's desire.

A few hours later several members of that body arrived at the palace, perhaps anticipating more mischief from the tyrant. But Herod's features wore a smile of feigned kindness and grace as he tried to mask the bloodthirsty thoughts of his heart. He soon made the men acquainted with what he wanted to know. "Tell me, my good men, where is the expected King of the Jews to be born, the King you are all speaking of and hoping for, the promised Messiah?" he asked.

If some of the scholars received the announcement with genuine wonder in their hearts, they did not show it by word or look, but they answered as best they could, "In Bethlehem, O King, according to the prophecy of Micah."

The simple answer of the learned men did not satisfy the tyrant's curiosity and growing anxiety. He wanted to know more. He wanted it clearly defined as to where and when this event would take place. If the scholars had been able to answer these questions, they probably would have done so, if only to multiply the fears of the ruler. But their knowledge about the matter was at this time too limited. Groaning with disappointment, the king waved his hand and dismissed the scholars.

After the last of the scribes had closed the door of the chamber behind him, Herod fell back in the bed, burying his face in the cushions, his talonlike fingers tearing at the silky fabric of the coverings. Caleb, beholding this, wished with all his heart to be far, far away. He expected the worst for himself. Only through the strength of his will was he able to control his quaking body. And his anxiety and fear were intensified as he beheld the look of triumph in the face of Limus, who stood as usual at the head of the bed. After a while Herod's groaning ceased, and as he began to look wildly about him, he glanced at the terror-stricken face of the wretched captain, who saw in the black orbs of the king the lust to kill. It drove him to his knees.

"Gracious king," he began to babble, "allow thy servant to speak." Encouraged by a slight nod from Herod, he continued, "To prove my loyalty to thee, O mighty King, I humbly beg permission to seek this vile pretender and fetch Him to face the wrath of my only rightful lord."

Untamed cruelty flashed in the monarch's eyes as he stared at the kneeling captain. But he only whispered, "If only I could trust you!"

Noting the king's suspicion and indecision, the desperate courtier hoped to reassure him by declaring, "I shall be worthy of the trust of my king. It is only for him to command."

Herod seemed not to hear, his smoldering eyes staring into space, as if recalling the eventful years of his treacherous reign. His actions and despicable deeds but told him that he had made few friends on whom he could depend. Because of his own selfish nature he never trusted anyone. Perhaps he was not to be blamed altogether for this, for the poorly veiled hatred of the people toward him had done little to improve his feeling toward them. And now, about seventy years old, he felt with bitterness that there was no one to whom he could look for help. The murderous flame died down in his eyes as he looked upon his hireling, and something almost akin to a change of heart was expressed in them as he said, "Your lips have spoken the words of a true servant, but still I distrust you. For your eyes tell me that you love me but little, and that you would greatly rejoice if I should be no more. And for this alone you deserve death. But I shall be merciful and shall forget your transgression, if only you will deliver this newborn King into my hands."

Caleb, feeling as if he had just wakened from a dream, began to rise on one knee, and with a fleeting glance at the darkening face of Limus, he said, "Thy mercy, gracious lord, overshadows the anger in thy heart, and I greatly rejoice to be thought worthy of doing thy will."

The king was little deceived by the captain's assertion, and told him as much as he dismissed him with the final warning, "Be you certain to remember this at all times."

After Caleb's departure, the three Magi, who had been

entertained and refreshed in a guest room of the castle, were again ushered into the king's presence. In vain did he try to get more definite news from them concerning the newborn King. Finally he dismissed them with the words, "Go and search diligently for the young Child, and when ye have found Him, bring me word again that I may also come and worship Him."

Soon afterwards the three men left. However sincere their promise to return may have been, their failure to keep faith with the king was part of the plan to defeat his treacherous design.

XIV

Nathan in Trouble

KNOWING he had to succeed or pay with his life if he failed, Caleb went in search of his quarry with desperate energy. But much to his great annoyance, he found not the slightest trace of the so-called newborn King. Wherever he went and whomever he asked, the answer was always the same: No one seemed to know or to have heard of such a one. For days and weeks he had his mercenaries on the move, scouting and searching all Bethlehem and its surroundings, but without success. He tried to find the three astrologers who had visited the palace, to force from them at least some information; but they seemed to have vanished. Despair mounted in his heart as he thought of the consequences of his failure to satisfy the king's growing suspicion about him.

One evening, returning from another day of fruitless search, Caleb entered his apartment, looking for a moment at Jesup with the hope of receiving some information from him, and threw himself, moaning, on the couch, when a gentle knock at the door brought him suddenly to the realization of his predicament. "It is Limus," his racing thoughts were telling him, "to fetch me for the reckoning!"

For a long moment he sat with blanched lips, his eyes seeking a way of escape, and then ordered Jesup to see who the visitor was. Obediently the servant opened the door and revealed the trembling form of Melchor the stableboy. With a sigh of profound relief the Idumean saw that it was not the king's valet; but this show of relief quickly changed to rage as he laid eyes on Melchor. Rising slowly from the couch, the heavy horsewhip gripped in his right hand, he shouted, "And since when have I given permission for a mere stable-boy to enter my apartment?" Annoyed by the menial's silence and hesitation, he angrily demanded, "Answer me, wretch, before I horsewhip you within an inch of your life!"

But the boy had eyes only for the whip, the sight of which forced him to his knees and loosened his tongue. "Noble master, O hear what I have to tell before you give me the punishment my actions so surely deserve. But I have news of the utmost importance for you," the boy stammered. Something in the tone of the boy's voice caused the captain to hesitate and to master for a moment his inner rage. Then he said, "News? What news could a stableboy bring that would be of interest to me? But speak and we shall see."

"The report of your fruitless search for the newborn King of the Jews, my gracious lord," the boy began, rising from his knees, "has come to my ears, and your reward for any information concerning Him has made me improperly bold. The desire to receive my freedom at your hands in exchange for knowledge of this King made me dare to seek you in your own apartment."

New hope possessed Caleb as he listened. His attitude toward the poor fellow suddenly changed. He ran to the boy, seized him by the shoulders and jerked him sharply over the threshold into the room, kicking the door shut behind them.

"Wine!" he shouted to his bewildered servant. "A cup of wine for my good friend Melchor, who indeed has brought me important news!"

Relief, joy, and anticipation were reflected in his voice as the captain took the cup filled to the brim with wine, and handed it to the puzzled hostler with the words, "Drink, my good man, drink to the freedom which you shall surely have if ever you lead me to this King."

Melchor seemed to have forgotten his desire for revenge
for the horsewhipping he had received only a fortnight ago
at the hands of the captain. His only thought now was to be
freed from the slavery which bound him to a cruel master.

After hurriedly swallowing the proffered cup of wine, the
boy explained how he happened to have information about
the newborn King of the Jews. He was ignorant of the fact
that his own death was planned for as soon as he had served
the captain's purpose. And a half hour later he left the
palace, accompanied by a score of Thracians, who were
ordered to assist him in the arrest of the shepherds. Caleb
never dreamed of the shock that was in store for him as he
watched from his window the departure of the little band.

Melchor was not familiar with the location of Asa's camp.
He knew only that it was located somewhere on the road to
Jericho. But by persistent inquiries from people he encountered on the way, he found himself, together with his escort,
in the vicinity of the camp by nightfall.

Nathan, alone at the camp, was in the act of preparing
his frugal supper when he became aware of the approach of
Melchor and his Thracians. Stepping guardedly outside the
hut, he looked with suspicion at the soldiers as they began
to surround it. A pang of fear shot through him as he thought
of his kinsmen. They were expected any minute from the
town, where they had gone at daybreak. He recognized the
band as one usually commanded by Caleb the Idumean. If
the thought of flight to sound a warning entered his mind,
he did not show it as he gazed at the band in silence, watchful and waiting.

At sight of the giant herder, Melchor thanked his good
fortune for having brought the Thracians with him to assist
him in his task, for the herder looked as if he indeed would

be a formidable opponent. Cautiously approaching, Melchor remained well beyond the reach of the mighty arms of the shepherd and asked politely, "Where are your kinsmen?"

A smile of loathing accompanied Nathan's answer as he replied, "Since when has it come to pass that a traitorous slave has the privilege of inquiring about free men?"

Nathan was well acquainted with Caleb's servant. He had seen him frequently at the market square of the town and had felt sorry for him, for he knew the circumstances that had brought about his bondage. The poor boy was taken in payment for some alleged debts, incurred to all appearances by his father, who had died at the hands of Caleb the Idumean.

For a moment the darkness prevented Nathan from seeing the blood rush to the boy's face. Pride and the hope of becoming a free man again made Melchor suppress the sense of guilt that had surged up in his young heart. Sure of the support that was behind him, he said boldly, "It is not I who am asking you for information of your kinsmen, but my master, the noble Caleb. He desires to have speech with them, and you would be wise to keep a civil tongue in your mouth."

Nathan ignored the warning, and his smile deepened at the corners of his mouth, as he replied, "And what, my good friend, could that business be that made it necessary to send you with an armed escort? Cannot I be of service to him without this show of force?"

Moved by the love he felt for his kinsmen, Nathan would have thought no sacrifice too great, if it would but serve the welfare of David and his family. But Melchor's next words dispelled any such hope as he might have nourished in his heart when he said, "This is not for me to decide. My orders are to bring you three men to the palace peaceably or, if necessary, by force. What happens after that will be no concern of mine."

The leader of the soldiers, six feet tall, a veteran of many skirmishes, had so far listened with patience to the exchange of the two Jews. But when he noticed the bold manner of the herder, the trooper thought it wise to intervene. Pushing the stableboy aside with a sweep of his powerful arm, he confronted Nathan, measured him with an insolent glance, and snapped cuttingly, "Speak up, you lout, tell what you know, or by the bones of my father, I will teach you better manners!"

Nathan fought the desire to smash the mocking face before him with his formidable fist, and said with defiance, "I answer you not, you carrion eater. You are not wise enough to teach your superiors better manners."

An expression of anger flared up in the Thracian's face as he derisively blurted out, "Ho, ho, my proud cockerel, spoken like a brave man, but you are none, for I can hear only the boast of a smelly mutton eater!" And with lightning swiftness he shot out his right hand, intending to come to grips with the herder. But the soldier had undervalued the fighting quality of his antagonist. Nathan anticipated the move and was prepared for it. Melchor stood amazed as he beheld the catlike speed and agility of his countryman, as the latter avoided the grasping hand of his adversary by ducking low and coming up between the outstretched arms of the rushing soldier. And with a move too quick for the eye, the herder's mighty arms were tightening around the middle of the Thracian. A viselike grip, then the sound of breaking bones. And before anyone really knew what had taken place, the lifeless form of the ruffian slipped from Nathan's relaxing arms.

All this happened so quickly that it was some time before

the soldiers realized they were looking at a dead man. But when they finally rushed in, Nathan gave ground. By the slight illumination of the little fire which he had built a few steps from the entrance of the hut to light the way for David and his father on their return from the town, the hard-pressed herder snatched the broadsword of his enemy from its scabbard with the thought of selling his life dearly if necessary.

It had not been his intention to kill the Thracian. He had merely wanted to teach him a lesson for his insolent words. He glanced now with sorrow and regret at the unexpected result of his attack. He knew only too well that from this moment on he would be a hunted man, a man wanted for murder.

XV

The Prisoners

A SA and his son David had left the sheep camp at early
dawn to pay a visit to Elizabeth and little Jonathan. They found the mother, almost well again,
busily engaged in giving the laughing and crowing
boy the usual morning bath, and they watched with glee his
mischievous actions, as his tiny hands and feet spattered the
water into his mother's face. And as she lifted him from the
little tub, made of sheepskins and resembling a large square
bag, its corners fastened to a four-posted wooden rig, and
laid him into the soft, clean linen of his small crib, Asa could
not resist the temptation to touch the child's rosy cheeks and
body, and as he looked steadily into the little face, he whispered, "God bless you, joy of my old days." All the love with
which his old heart was filled for the grandson he had longed
for shone in the face of the old man.

During the remainder of the day Asa could be seen sitting
on a little footstool close to the crib, watching and passing
the time with the clear-eyed boy. He even ventured to look
at the birthmark, and as he recalled for a fleeting moment
that he had once cherished the hope that the little boy might
be the promised Messiah, a feeling of self-reproach at the
thought faintly flushed his face.

David felt a deep joy in his heart as he thus beheld his
father so happy and contented. But the long shadows of
eventide had drawn nigh, and with them came the hour for
departure. When Elizabeth, with her little son pressed to
her breast, waved farewells from the doorway till a bend in

the road hid them from her view, she little knew how final
that last farewell was to be.

An hour or so later, David, approaching the camp a few
yards ahead of his father, stopped suddenly and listened.
The sound of swordplay and the groans of wounded men
came distinctly to his sensitive ears. Asa, whose hearing was
somewhat impaired, looked questioningly at his son and inquired, "What is it, my son, that troubles you?"

David did not seem to hear, but hastened the rest of
the way up to the camp, his heart suddenly filled with a
terrible premonition of disaster when he observed flame and
smoke that signified more than a mere campfire. Reaching
the brow of the hill upon which their camp was situated, the
young herder beheld a scene that surpassed his darkest fears.
The cabin was aflame, and by the illumination of the burning
hut David made out the towering form of Nathan trying to
defend himself against a number of mercenaries from the
palace. He had no idea why or how long the unequal struggle
had been going on. Only one thought possessed him at the
moment, to spring to the aid of his hard-pressed friend. But
the restraining hand of his father prevented him from doing
so. His sharp eye was quick to see the futility of his son's
intended action.

"Son, keep your head, and let me handle this. There are
too many of them even against you and Nathan. I shall try to
draw their attention away from our kinsman to give him a
chance to escape from them," the old herder said to restrain
his impetuous son. David followed the advice of his father
and waited.

Asa, putting two fingers to his lips, sent into the night a
shrill whistle which could be heard above the noise of the
struggle. At the sound of the familiar signal, Nathan jerked
his head up, his battle-lit eyes searching for his friends. His

thoughts for the moment centering only on the safety of his kinsmen, he momentarily relaxed his guard against attack from behind. The warning cry of David was heard too late, and the gleaming dagger of a Thracian, who had quietly come up behind the giant, was thrust into the back of the unsuspecting herder.

The stricken Nathan tried with extreme effort to warn the onrushing David of the danger and disaster awaiting him and Asa at the hand of Caleb the Idumean, but the exertion was too much for him. His mind was benumbed, his mighty legs began to buckle, and with a heavy thud he fell, face down to the ground before the burning hut.

Stunned and grief-stricken, David threw himself down beside the lifeless form of his kinsman, desperately seeking in him some sign of life.

The stableboy watched all this with terror and consternation. The face of the slain man aroused a terrible sense of guilt in the boy's heart. And as he glanced at Asa, who had stepped to the side of his kneeling son, Melchor profoundly regretted the terms of his bargain for release from Caleb, but not for long. To his great relief from deep remorse, he sought and found a satisfying extenuation for his part in this most unfortunate affair. "How dreadful was the price he had to pay for it! But," so he reasoned, "is it really my fault that this man was slain? Did he not first kill the Thracian?"

Presently regarding himself as wholly innocent, he disclaimed all responsibility and, as he stepped a little closer to the old man, boldly declared, "The death of this foolish kinsman of yours was his own fault. He only received the due reward for his own actions. The soldiers slew him because of the murder of their leader."

David, infuriated by the words of the boy, gently laid the blood-covered head of his dead friend on the ground, quickly rose from his knees, and faced the impudent Jew. "And why, you miserable wretch, did my kinsman slay this infidel? Answer me this, or I shall strangle you with these my own hands!"

Melchor retreated in fear, understanding only too well the feeling of the young herder. But not a word came to his bloodless lips. David, interpreting the silence as a sign of guilt, gave vent to his intense fury. "Turncoat and traitor, whatever you receive as a reward for this night's affair, it shall taste forever as gall in your lying mouth, for this I know, whatever my dead friend did, he was justified in doing it," David shouted at the trembling stableboy.

Melchor, almost instantly recovering from his first shock of fear, countered arrogantly, "I care little about your opinion of me, and I tell you again that I had no part in the death of this rash fool. All I asked of him was that he tell me where I could find you and your father, for my master, Captain Caleb, desired your presence at the palace." Then stopping for a moment, he added, "And if you are wise, you will take heed and come willingly. It will be to your advantage."

David stood for a long moment to contemplate his dilemma, weighing the words of the slave, then suffered his hands to be bound by one of the soldiers. As he glanced at his dazed father, standing motionless at his side, he felt like screaming into the black night the terrible woe and misery that filled his soul. In the dim light of the dying fire, as he looked about, David spied Caleb the dog, a dagger in his ribs, lying dead at the side of the fallen Nathan.

The body of the slain leader of the Thracians was placed on a crude makeshift stretcher hastily put together from the strong limbs of a stunted oak that had stood for years like a sentinel on the brow of the hill; and lifting it to their shoulders, two of the Thracian guardsmen fell into line behind Melchor as he gave the signal for the return to the palace.

Asa and David, guarded by a soldier on each side, lingered for a brief moment to take a last look at Nathan, who was lying immobile beside the dying embers of the cabin. Then they followed the troopers into the night. Their thoughts ran in the same direction. Both were convinced of the fact that their arrest was only a forerunner of more dreadful events to come, and regretted bitterly not having finished off the captain when they once had had the opportunity to do so.

The gray-haired old herder walked behind his son like a man stupified. His lips were moving, and he was blaming himself for the terrible tragedy at the camp. If he had not whistled, he argued to himself, Nathan surely would not have become distracted, and would have fought on, despite tremendous odds, and perhaps would have escaped. On his wrinkled forehead large beads of sweat gathered as his tortured mind tried to dispel the fog and chaos that beclouded his thoughts. This had all happened so suddenly. Only a few hours ago he had sat in the little home at Bethlehem with his loved ones, rejoicing at the sight of his grandson. Full contentment then filled his breast, for he felt that everything he had hoped for had come to pass.

David had not spoken a word since he had been bound by the soldier. He thought of his wife and child. What would become of them? He harbored no false hope, nor did he deceive himself as to the seriousness of their situation, knowing their arrest had been instigated by the vengeful Caleb. He became even more disturbed as he thought of his father, who walked moaning behind him. "What about him?" David's thoughts ran. "Why should he suffer for an affair in which he had no part?" recalling to mind the terrible beating which he himself had given the Idumean. Both herders were ignorant of the real reason for their being taken into custody.

David attempted several times to speak to his father, but each time was prevented from doing so by the guard at his side. Desperation gripped his soul, for he saw no means of escape, as the ominous outline of the fortress now loomed out of the night. "Why," he asked himself, "cannot I think of some way that would help to free my father? He still would be able to take care of Elizabeth and little Jonathan."

A few minutes later the bound herders were marched through the portal of the mighty gate and rushed to the guardhouse, where a special guard was assigned to watch over them. Melchor, knowing his prisoners secured, was about to leave the guardroom to report to his master, when a husky Thracian with a battle-scarred face grasped him by the shoulder, turning him around. "Is this your newborn King in swaddling clothes?" the veteran said mockingly to the frightened stableboy, and pointed at the stalwart figure of David. "By the great Jupiter, if it is, he certainly has grown fast!"

A riotous burst of laughter broke from the deep throats of the soldiers, who were lounging about the spacious room as they listened to the joke of their sergeant. With a helpless gesture the horseboy turned toward the door and beheld the haughty Caleb as he slowly entered the room.

David, who was partly hidden by his father's broad back, for a moment escaped the eye of the captain. A diabolical smile of triumph shone in the face of the latter as he stepped to Asa's side. Rubbing his hands in unholy glee, he said, "This is indeed a surprise to behold you, my noble friend, so soon again. Fear not, I have not forgotten you and our little interview on the road!"

If the captain expected to see an expression of fear come to the face of Asa, he certainly was disappointed, for the cold and expressionless stare from the herder's eye told him nothing. Looking at the crowing Idumean with a trace of loathing, Asa replied softly, but with a steady voice, "Your hour of triumph has arrived. I am in your power. But I fear you little, for my soul and my thoughts are still my own!"

At this moment the captain spied the motionless David and answered with deadly meaning, "Your mouth is bigger than your head, for you speak foolishly. Be assured of this: I would break your stiff neck quickly, if I had not received an order to deliver both of you to my gracious king!"

The soldiers, standing around the group, were looking with something akin to respect at the defiant face of Asa; but as they followed the sharp words of the captain, their mocking grins told him of the joy which they derived from the affair. To hide his rising anger, Caleb turned to Melchor and asked, "Did you not inform me that there were three of them? Why do my eyes behold only two?" As no immediate answer came from the frightened boy, he thundered, "Speak up! Where is the third one?"

"He is no more, my lord" the boy stammered. "He is dead. He was slain when he refused to do thy will, and because he killed big Bardia."

Melchor's story was soon verified by the soldiers who were present at the arrest. Enraged by the news, Caleb, with a dark and sinister gleam in his eyes, glared intently at the two captive shepherds. Then he left the room.

XVI

Before Herod

CALEB found the king in an ugly mood. Limus the Greek had just filled the golden drinking cup which the irascible ruler had emptied several times. His unsteady gaze centered on the slowly approaching captain; and when he recognized his officer, he dashed the full cup to the floor, splattering the contents over himself and the bed. Infuriated at the sight of the captain, Herod shouted, "Dog, who called you in here? Do you seek to know whether I am still alive? Well, I am. And you will know it soon enough! For my patience with you has come to an end!"

The venomous sneer of the valet told the trembling Caleb how much help he could expect from the servant, and Caleb cursed his own stupidity for not having disposed of the vile knave at the first opportunity. After a deliberate silence of painfully long minutes, the king granted the captain permission to speak, who in a few words informed the king of the arrest and custody of the herders.

"What are you waiting for, you stupid fool!" Herod stormed. "Bring them in here!"

A moment later Asa and David entered the room, bowing low before the king. At a wave of the royal hand, all the guards retired except two husky fellows from Gaul, who took their position behind the two hapless Jews. Three scholarly looking men with impressive charts and scrolls of papers tucked under their arms stood like shadows in a corner of the bedchamber. These were Herod's favorite astrologers. A foppishly dressed little man with a varied array of bottles and jars before him on a tray attempted to hide his anger and disgust from the watchful eye of the valet. He was the king's barber. Having finished his work, he had been waiting several hours for permission to leave the room. It was the king's custom to tantalize his court servants in this manner. Robbed most of the time of sleep and healthful rest by the pain and remorse of vice and debauchery, the king found immense pleasure in calling any of his subjects at any hour of the day or night. The sight of their discomfort would often relieve his own misery.

The eyes of the tyrant rested for a long time on the stoic features of the prisoners. His look was one of appraisal and calculation. At last he turned to the captain and cried, "Why are these men bound? How dare you bind any of my subjects, and especially these men who are bearers of good tidings? Release them this very moment!"

Without comprehending the strange and unexpected order of the king, Caleb hastened to obey. Asa and David, however, were not deceived by this apparent show of unwonted friendliness. Too many were the tales they both had heard of the cunning and hypocritical ways of the old fox. Although they did not know what to expect, it became clear to them now that their trouble was with Herod and not with Caleb. But only David had an inkling as to what it was all about.

"Come, my good men, be not afraid, and step closer," Herod encouraged the herders after they had been freed from their bonds. Hesitatingly they drew closer to the bed. Reclining in the soft silk cushions, the king continued with a smile, "I have sent for you to answer only one question, and if the answer is satisfactory I will reward you richly and set you free again."

Asa answered humbly, "Speak, O King, that we may obey."

With a smile playing at the corners of his mouth, the king looked at the venerable Asa and said, "You are a wise man, and out of respect for your age I shall not prolong the interview; I shall be brief and direct. Where can I find the newborn King of the Jews, whom you had the privilege to worship at His birth?" Seeing the herder's hesitation, the king continued, "I am an old man; my life is far spent, and my only desire is to see this newborn King and to worship Him."

Still Asa did not answer, but the angry flush rising in the king's face told him he must decide quickly. The reply could not be long withheld. Under no condition would he tell what he knew, and he took it for granted that David had likewise so resolved. Certainly the prospect of being free again, if only for the sake of Elizabeth and her child, was almost irresistibly persuasive. But the price would be too great—it would be the end of his beloved King and Messiah! No, he would not, he could not answer. Rather die a thousand deaths than betray the hope and faith of his enslaved people!

The long silence of the herder began to irk the short-tempered ruler. "Come, come, my good fellow," the king commanded, as he suddenly sat bolt upright in the bed, "speak up and try not my patience." When no answer came, he began to rage furiously. "Dogs! How dare you defy my wish? Do you not know that I can have you slain for not giving me answer?" And then, taking a deep breath, he turned to the captain. "Bind them again and send me Ja'bes, and we shall see if we cannot loosen their tongues."

Caleb was glad to obey the king's order. Making a rapid exit, he returned almost instantly with Ja'bes, the king's private executioner. Slowly he entered the room, his beady little eyes resting for a moment on the two bound men. His arms, abnormally long and reaching below his knees, were covered with a growth of reddish hair. Greasy, uncombed red hair hanging in strings over a low forehead almost touched the bushy eyebrows of the same color, which continued in a straight line above a flat nose with prominent nostrils. But it was the mouth that held the attention of the herders. The upper lip was drawn back as if in a snarl, showing discolored yellow teeth, which resembled the fangs of an animal. Bound around his loins was the skin of a leopard. His walk was the rolling gait of an ape, and, if seen in the dark, he might easily have been mistaken for one.

A motion from Herod brought Ja'bes to the bedside, where the king whispered a few words to him. With an apelike contortion, the creature uttered an inhuman terrifying sound. It was the fiendish glee of a savage beast, ready to pounce upon its prey. Saliva drooled from the corners of the cruel mouth as the executioner listened to his master. The herders did not know that the fellow was without a tongue. Herod had ways of guarding his secrets—he made certain of the silence of his tools!

David's mind was in a turmoil as he looked at his old father. Instead of the accustomed light of happiness in the aged man's eyes, his son observed a cold and almost lifeless stare. David had a premonition that he and his old father would never leave the fortress alive.

Before Herod gave the signal for Ja'bes to proceed with the torture, he addressed the herders once more, giving them the choice of freedom and riches, or torture and death. And to his great surprise Asa began to speak, saying, "I have heard thy offer, O King, and I am ready to answer thee. By the truth of Heaven, to thee is given the power to do with me whatever is thy desire. Thou canst throw me into the deepest dungeon of this fortress, so that I may nevermore behold the golden rays of the sun. Thou canst even take from me my life. But," Asa now continued with growing courage, "thou hast not the power to force me to betray this newborn King. I fear not the torture. I have lived my life, and thou art able to take from it only a short span of the time allotted to me."

The evil thoughts that were at work behind the clouded brow of the raging king found expression as he said, "Son of a swine, you shall regret your daring words!" As he spoke, he appeared as one possessed. His fiendish eyes, glancing around the room, came to rest on the ugly form of his executioner. David, missing nothing, noticed with a shudder the slight nod of the king's head, and leaped forward to shield his old father, resolved to fight for him to the end.

Over Ja'bes' face came a gleam of joy. The lust and pleasure which he felt in performing his fiendish acts were manifest in every move of his body. The viselike fingers of his right hand were gripping the stock of a whip (a cat-o'-nine-tails) that consisted of nine heavy strips of leather with small lead weights imbedded in its ends,—a murderous weapon, especially in the hands of Ja'bes.

David waited, every nerve of his body taut, ready for instant action. Coming closer and closer to the herders, Ja'bes' hairy arm shot up as if to strike. But he never completed the downward stroke, for the young herder's feet leaped from the floor and sank with the force of two mighty pistons into the abdomen of the butcher, and with a weird cry of pain the creature went down, his gorillalike arms and hands beating the floor in terrifying motion. He tried to rise, but even the stern command of Herod was of no avail, for the fellow was completely paralyzed. As the ruler looked from his prostrate henchman to the poised figure of David, who was still manacled, something akin to admiration stole into his face. He was probably recalling the days when he himself had once enjoyed the thrill and challenge of deadly combat and danger. But the reprieve of the prisoners was short-lived. At Herod's command, David was thrown to the floor by the two mercenaries and shackled hand and foot.

XVII

Asa Dies

WITH a look of contempt at the groaning Ja'bes, Herod ordered Caleb to remove the fellow to his own quarters. The guards obeyed quickly, and after they had left the room with their charge, Herod, pointing to one of the braziers filled with glowing charcoal, commanded the captain, "Have yonder basin moved over here to my side, and I will break the stubborn will of this old goatherd."

A devilish smile formed at the corners of Herod's mouth as he noted the look of affection which the old herder gave his son. Asa's pride in his son David was justified by the love and loyalty which he had always shown for his father. And on this fact Herod began to build his hope of getting at the secret of the herders. Herod seemed to have read the mind of Asa as he once more spoke to him. "Tell me, is this your only son?" he inquired brusquely.

Wondering what the king's motive behind the question might be, Asa answered, "Yes, your majesty."

Satisfied with the answer, Herod continued, "And would you not do anything in your power to save him from harm?"

"O King, that I would," Asa replied in a voice that was warm with affection for his son.

The king leaned closer to the old man and said softly, almost seductively, "Come, tell me where I can find this King." And interpreting the expression in Asa's face as one of fear and indecision, he grew more persistent as he added, "My good fellow, great shall be your reward, exceeding even your fondest hopes. Only tell me."

Asa, looking at the hypocrite, fought the desire to spit into the royal face, knowing only too well that his life would be forfeited whether he told or not, and said, "My answer, O King, is still the same. I will never tell thee, so ask me no more."

Those in the room—the three astrologers, the barber, who still stood beside the mischievous valet, and the frightened captain—marveled at the courage displayed by the herder. "This fellow is mad," Caleb thought, "or he is ignorant of what is in store for him."

For a moment it seemed as if the King faltered as his mounting rage sought expression. The blood rushed wildly to his face, and his talonlike fingers were tearing to shreds the silk cover of the bed. Finally, pointing with shaking finger to the dagger in the courtier's girdle, he shouted at the shivering captain, "Give me that dagger." And when Caleb hesitated, he repeated madly, "Give it to me or I will have your head!" The ashen-faced captain drew the weapon from his girdle and handed it quickly to the king. "Throw this dog over here, and I will prove to them that I am still their king, their only king." The two guards silently obeyed and flung the helpless David beside the king's bed, where the two guards held him firmly to the floor.

With a deliberate slowness designed to indicate and intensify the cruelty of his threat, Herod poised the needle-sharp dagger over David's eyes. When the king noted that the herders were still adamant in their refusal to betray the secret, he forthwith thrust the weapon into David's left eye.

"Now are you ready to tell?" the mad king shrieked, "or shall I busy myself with the other eye?"

David's father was stricken with grief and terror as he, helpless, witnessed the deed of monstrous cruelty. When Asa,

horrified and silent, refused by word or other sign to stay
the hand of the king, Herod almost executed the threatened
stroke that would have left David forever sightless. However, the king, exhausted by the rage and effort, fell back
half-conscious into the pillows, and, strangely enough, not
one of his attendants stirred to calm or assist him; neither
did they attempt to silence the old herder as he stood beside
his prostrate son and, without any thought of the consequences, poured out upon the faintly protesting Herod a
torrent of rebuke and invective that stunned the king and
his courtiers.

"Thou son of an infidel, thou art truly a spawn of the evil
powers, for thou knowest no other will but thine own! But
hear me. By the will of a God Eternal, it is I who am chosen
to curse thy black soul to hell for the thing done to my only
son, the joy of my old days! No, do not try to stop me, for I
will not be silenced. Well do I know that my end is near. I
know this from the deadly hatred in thine eyes. But I care
not. Before I die, I will speak to thee as one chosen by the
will of my people, a people enslaved by thee, and not, as it
appeared, by the will of the Romans. They at least have
respected our sacred customs. Nor have they openly despised
our way of worship. Neither can it be said of them that they
have made the office of our high priest a place of merchan-
dising and low intrigue."

Asa paused, his stare fixed on the shaking ruler, and then
continued, "Thou art an old man. Yet peace and contentment
were ever a stranger to thy wicked soul. Bond of blood and
love did not stay thy bloody hand as it slew the fair and
noble Mariamne and her sons. The hope of my suffering
people, to be ruled again some day by a grandson of the
noble Hyrcanus, vanished forever with this thy wicked act.
Thou hast offered me riches and freedom if I would deliver

this newborn King into thy hands. Oh, how little dost thou know a true son of Abraham! If I had a hundred lives to give, gladly would I sacrifice them all for the welfare of this King and Messiah to my people of Israel."

The king's body quivered as he felt the burning eyes of the old herder pierce his black soul. Asa, with rising fervor in his voice, went on, "I stand before thee a poor herder, an ignorant man. Yet I have witnessed the ruination and wanton destruction of my beloved land by thy parasites and spittle-lickers, who have taken the places of our counselors and teachers, who were ever willing to serve the welfare of their countrymen. Thy reign of blood and terror has come to its very end. Thou reapest as thou hast sown. A curse from the lips of an ignorant herder, who speaks to thee without fear, is thy reward."

The king attempted to raise his hand to silence the shepherd, but it dropped to his side as if paralyzed. And in his glittering eyes shone a flash of terror. His trembling hand flew to his face as if to shut out the thoughts which the old Jew's words so vividly brought to his mind.

But the old herder had ceased speaking, and utter silence reigned throughout the room again. Herod scanned the circle of faces before him, and madness gripped him anew as he encountered the defiant stare from the old man's eyes. Then, mustering all the strength at his command, he suddenly reached above his head, took down a slender-shafted jereed, his favorite weapon, from the wall, and hurled it with unerring aim at the naked breast of Asa, who fell backward to the floor.

"That is how much I fear your curse. You will never have the pleasure to witness my death, for I myself will kill you!" the king shrieked.

The maniac was a dreadful picture to behold as he swayed

in the bed like a drunken man, watching with satanical glee the futile efforts of his victim to dislodge the lance.

Failing in this effort, Asa gave up the struggle and lay still in order to husband the little strength left in his body, and gazed with pathetic, sorrowing eyes on the prone figure of his son. The intense desire to speak once more to his son gave him the strength to raise his head and utter his last words: "My son, do not betray the Savior of our people, but believe in Him, for He will be your strength and refuge in the days to come." And with a last low moan, the herder's head fell back to the floor and lay still in death!

The astrologers and the king's barber stood horror-stricken as they watched the sudden turn of the affair and waited anxiously for the signal to leave the bedchamber. Fear for their own safety was written in their faces. Even the callous Caleb, ever inclined to use force in obtaining any desired end, felt his spirit shaken within him as he beheld his former enemy dead before him. True, he could not be accused of the old fellow's death, yet he blamed himself for it, since he had instigated the arrest which led directly to it. His guilty conscience would never let him forget the herder's curse.

The harsh voice of the king broke in upon his thoughts and brought him quickly to the realization that despite the sordid affair of the day Herod had not abandoned his pursuit of the newborn pretender to the Idumean throne. Momentarily the inquisition of David would be resumed with redoubled cruelty.

XVIII

David's Faithfulness

HEROD gave orders for the removal of the dead herder from the room, his smoldering eyes on the pain-racked David. His warped brain could not comprehend the reason for their silence or their readiness to forfeit freedom and life rather than give up their secret.

By birth an Arab, but in conversation and manners a Greek, playing the game of politics whenever he saw fit to secure for himself the favor and good will of Caesar, Herod had very little time to study the hearts and minds of the people over whom he was appointed to rule. Yet he was conscious of the fact that he was despised by his subjects and that he was not regarded by them with the degree of respect to which he felt himself entitled. There had been a time, however, when he courted their good will, as when, for instance, he built for them a most magnificent house of worship, the Temple.

This Temple was indeed a marvel of architectural beauty, sitting majestically on the summit of Mount Moriah. With its marble colonnades forming the Porch of Solomon on the eastern side, and the Court of the Gentiles on the southern side, it became the gathering place of the people, whether young or old, from Jerusalem or far-off places. Over the broad marble floors of the colonnades one could see people strolling at leisure, could see the venerable rabbis holding school, and could watch the transaction of business by the traders and money-changers.

Herod went even further in his effort to win the people's heart by building a theater and a circus arena at Jerusalem, thus enabling the younger people to seek pleasure at the games. Yet he had but little success in all these efforts, for his despotic temperament and his inability to appreciate the traditional values of the Jews prevented a cordial relationship between himself and the people. To them he was still an upstart, a politician who had by devious devices wormed himself into the good graces of imperial Rome. His fanatical love for Greek art and culture was always shown at his court, filled with Greek parasites, philosophers, and scholars, who were anathema to the religious nationalism of his alien subjects.

The ever-growing taxes which he levied upon the people for the maintenance of his luxurious court had brought the long-suffering and patience of the people to the verge of open rebellion against him. But the hope for the manifestation of the long-awaited Messiah grew more and more in their hearts and had caused them to hold their peace and to endure the atrocities of the tyrant.

Angered by the failure of the Magi to return to Jerusalem with the information he so eagerly desired, and successfully thwarted in his other efforts to find the newborn King, Herod vented his mounting wrath upon the obstinately silent David, with whom he was about to resume his inquisitional interview.

Herod's mind was busy as he studied the mutilated face of his young prisoner, which reflected undying hatred and unfathomable anguish. His sorrow was so great that it stunned him into silence. He had never dreamed that it could come to this. He had anticipated torture and imprisonment, but never anything that would rob him of his father.

At the sight of the gloating face above him, he resolved

to make himself a son worthy of his venerable father. He would never tell! And as for his wife and little son, the mercy of the Lord would see to their safety and care. For had not his father's last words said as much—that the Lord would be his strength and refuge in the days to come?

It seemed at the moment that his thoughts and hopes might be justified, for Herod sank slowly back in the bed, exhausted. His strength, supported though it was by an iron will, forsook him, and only the nervous flicker in the piercing black eyes showed that his crafty brain was still at work, planning and scheming.

Feeling the need for rest, he ordered David removed to a dungeon. "But," he warned Caleb, "treat him well, for I promise more success with him next time, else he shall die a thousand deaths!"

His promise, however, bore little fruit, for no degree of torture could open the lips of the young herder, as he was brought again before the king a few days later. Seeing his plans thus frustrated and his last hope fade because of the stubbornness of the Jew, Herod lost all sense of reasoning and gave orders that the poor herder be blinded in the other eye.

And after this fiendish act was accomplished by his hench-man, he turned once more to the bleeding, tortured victim and cried, "I have spared your life for this purpose only, to prove to you that your refusal to speak was in vain, for I shall yet get my hands on Him whom you so valiantly have pro-tected. I shall slay every male child in Bethlehem from the age of two years down to the youngest, and thy King will not escape me!"

Not in the slightest manner did David show the anguish and sorrow that filled his heart at the madman's words. A moment of deepest despair swept over him, as he thought of his wife and child in Bethlehem. Would they be able to escape the murderous hand of the inhuman monster? Great drops of sweat appeared on his face as he tried to free himself from his bonds to get his bare hands on the insanely laughing king. But the exertion was too much for his torture-weakened body. With a cry, hardly human, David fell back and lay still as one dead.

XIX

Elizabeth in Despair

THE young wife of David could not understand why her loved ones had not returned from the camp. A whole week went by, and still no one came. She became worried, and a premonition of disaster filled her heart, especially so when she thought of Caleb the Herodian.

One evening, a few days later, as she stood in the door, looking along the caravan road for some sign of her husband's return, she decided to go herself or to send someone to the camp to find out what was wrong. Pressing little Jonathan close to her breast, she left the house and went over to the home of Lea, her neighbor, to seek her advice and help.

The elderly woman tried to quiet the young woman's fear. "Why do you worry about him?" she said. "I pity the fellow who dares arouse the anger of David."

But Elizabeth could not be comforted. She felt that something terrible had happened at the camp. It was not David's way to leave her so long without sending some word of himself.

Lea began to realize the seriousness of the situation and felt sorry for the poor woman. But what could she do to help? Soon the door opened, and in the doorway stood her son Uli. The face of the young boy was flushed from the exertion of running, and his eyes were filled with fear and excitement. Hastily closing the door behind him, the boy leaned with his back against it and fixed his eyes on the visitors.

"What is it, my son? Why are you so breathless?" Lea asked with a worried look. The boy hesitated to answer, but kept looking at little Jonathan. Lea, not knowing what to make of this, said excitedly, "Why do you not answer me? Is there something our friend here should not know about?"

The boy shook his head and said, "Mother, I am afraid that what I have to tell will hurt Elizabeth. But she must be told."

Bewildered, the woman, with a slight hesitation in her voice, asked, "Son, what are you speaking of? I do not understand the meaning of your words."

Then the boy related his story, telling how he had seen a band of soldiers in the town, entering and searching every house. "And mother," the excited Uli went on, "these soldiers are from the palace. I know the devils. They are not Romans. They are looking for all the little babies to kill them, in the hope of doing away with the newborn King of the Jews. I remembered little Jonathan, and ran as fast as I could to give Elizabeth time to hide somewhere with him before they could reach her house."

The two women stood terrified for a moment after the boy ceased speaking. But a commotion heard from the lower slope of the hill brought the young mother to the realization of the peril which threatened her little Jonathan. Pressing him closer to her breast, she ran to the door, crying out to her friend, "They shall never lay their bloody hands on my son! Never! For I will go to the camp. David will know how to protect his own from the hands of the murderers!"

As she left the house of her friend, she saw some of the mercenaries at the foot of the hill. Her only thought was to escape unseen. But she must go back to her own house once more. She needed a wrap for the little fellow to protect him against the chill of the coming night.

A few moments later she left the little cottage by the back

door, her sandaled feet hurrying over a short cut in the road that enabled her quickly to leave the town behind her. An hour later she was still pressing on. But her hurried step soon became a plodding walk. Her frail body and delicate constitution were not capable of withstanding the hardships of the strenuous trip. The poor, fear-driven woman had overestimated her strength. Darkness began to fall, blotting out the familiar landmarks by which she hoped to find the camp; and the feeling of being alone with her child in the open fields, as she listened with trembling heart to the fearsome noises of the night, almost caused her to cry out in despair. The thought of losing her way approached hysteria. Her eyes strained ahead, trying to find the stunted oak, at which she knew she would have to turn off the road to reach the camp. Would she ever see it? Or had she passed it?

The weight of her child was a severe strain on her limited strength. Her feet were like leaden weights as she trudged wearily on and on. Tears of despair dimmed her eyes as her exhausted body began to falter. The anguish and fear she had undergone the previous week had affected her waning strength.

Again her mind wandered to the vengeance-seeking Caleb. Perhaps her David was dead! The thought drove her on again, praying and hoping. But soon she stopped again; her strength, even her power of will, had left her. Sitting on a boulder that lay by the road, she gave way to tears and despair.

She knew now that she had lost her way and that there was no living soul near by to show her the road. And, as if to make her misery more intense, little Jonathan began to cry. She tried to go on but could not. For a moment she thought of sleeping until morning, but she dismissed this thought at once, for this, she feared, might mean the death of her little son.

How long she remained seated on the boulder she never knew, for suddenly she heard the sound of galloping horses. Jumping up, she stood rigid, her eyes trying to pierce the dark cover of the night. Two horsemen loomed before her, only a few hundred yards away. Supposing them to be some of the butchers from the Palace, the frantic woman tried to run from them; but her feet would not move. Her knees began to sag, and she crumpled slowly to the dust-covered road. She did not know that help for her had arrived.

XX

Marcus to the Rescue

THE two riders were Marcus and his bosom friend Silvanus, a centurion of the Roman garrison stationed at Carthage, who only a few days before had arrived at Jerusalem. Their friendship was of long standing. They had grown up together, and when young Marcus decided to join the army, Silvanus, rather than be separated from his friend, readily forfeited a life of ease and comfort and joined with him.

Their friendship became a byword at the army camps. They were always seen close to each other. They lived and loved and fought side by side, and were always satisfied with their lot. Nothing ever seemed to interfere with their feeling of strong mutual affection; and this was true even when they became acquainted with dark-eyed Leonia, the daughter of a wealthy wine merchant of Rome. Each one sought the favor of the beautiful maiden, and in the end this favor was bestowed upon the blue-eyed, blond-haired Marcus. Silvanus, the dark-visaged giant, accepted the decision with a smile of disappointment, and it seemed for a time as if their long standing friendship might come to an end. But such was not the case. The roots of their love and trust in each other had grown too deep to fail in this severe test of friendship.

Silvanus' love and admiration for the beautiful woman never died, but he was careful to conceal his feeling. This endeared the fellow more and more to their hearts; and Marcus and Leonia were ever careful to avoid even the slightest allusion that might evoke poignant memories.

Silvanus had been away from Jerusalem a little over a year, helping to quell an uprising at Carthage. Upon his return he was most heartily welcomed by the two friends. After expressing their joy at meeting each other again, they turned their conversation to Asa and his family, and Silvanus was pleasantly surprised to hear of the birth of little Jonathan.

A few hours later, as Marcus and Silvanus were strolling through the army camp and Marcus was speaking of his fear for the safety of their friends, Silvanus, the rash and impulsive one, burst out heatedly, "Why do we not go and pull the fangs out of this dog Caleb? Then all the worry for our friends would come to an end."

Marcus smiled understandingly and said, "Yes, we could do this if the wily fox would only come out into the open on some dark night when the danger of discovery would not be so great. But," continued Marcus, shrugging his shoulders with a gesture expressive of doubt, "you probably know as well as I do that the big he-wolf would be greatly upset if anything should happen to his favorite." They did not know that the captain was at this time very much in disfavor at the palace.

Catching the sound of an approaching horseman, Silvanus glanced for a moment toward the main road, which was only a short distance from the army post. It was almost dark, and the cool breeze blowing over the ridge of the southern hill made him wish for the cloak he had left at his quarters in Jerusalem.

Both men turned as a rider pulled his snorting mount to an abrupt stop before them, and a cry of welcome broke from Silvanus' lips as he recognized a familiar face. "By the cups of Bacchus, if it is not Julian, the friend of the grave-diggers!" the soldier mocked, greeting the newcomer. And grasping the stubby little fellow's hand, Silvanus shook it with a viselike grip that made Julian wince.

"Stop it, you lummox!" the little army surgeon wailed, jerking his hand from the iron grip of his friend. "You will break it!" And disregarding the good-natured laughter of the two soldiers, he continued, "Some day, my big boy, I shall be the friend of the gravediggers when they carry you into my tent on a stretcher!"

Marcus, well aware of the reciprocal respect of the two men, could not resist the inclination to ruffle further the quick temper of the little man, and said, "Why, my good Julian, do you not avoid him, knowing from experience that you are no match for him?"

"How was I to know that it was Silvanus," the little man sputtered, "I thought he was at Carthage. And besides, I did not offer to shake hands; my gentle friend was too quick for me."

The two soldiers laughed to observe the little man's pretended anger as he was trying to hide his real joy at the unexpected meeting. But their happy laughter ended suddenly when the surgeon pointed a stubby little finger at the distant palace and said, "The monster from over there is on the rampage again, for his bloody guardsmen are slaughtering every male child in the town from the age of two down to the youngest infant!" Observing the incredulity in their eyes, he continued heatedly, "I am telling you the truth, for my own eyes have seen it!"

When Marcus heard these words, his thoughts sped to David and little Jonathan, and he made a quick decision. "Come, Silvanus," he cried with deadly purpose in his voice, "let us ride. Perhaps it is still not too late to prevent the worst." Silvanus needed no urging, for he was close behind Marcus as the latter was running toward the stables for a mount.

Driven as if by Providence, Marcus, instead of taking the main road, took a short cut which he knew would bring him near the sheep camp of old Asa. As the riders neared the road that led to the camp, Silvanus pulled his horse to a sudden stop and cried warningly to Marcus, "Watch out, there is something in the road ahead of us!"

The warning was not needed, for Marcus, already out of the saddle, was advancing toward the object lying in the road. Cautiously bending over it, he was taken aback at the sight he beheld.

"By the great Pollus, it is a woman with her baby!" he whispered excitedly to his friend and then began to fume at the darkness that prevented his seeing more clearly. A moan from the woman's lips mingled with the feeble wail of the baby.

Silvanus, standing close by the side of the kneeling Marcus, asked, "Who is she? And what are we going to do with her?"

"I cannot make out who she is," Marcus answered softly. "Probably a poor creature from the town who managed to escape the butchers from the fortress. Let us try to be of some help to her. Here, you hold the child, and I shall see about the woman."

But before he could execute his well-meant intention, Elizabeth recovered from her swoon. Seeing the helmeted heads of the two soldiers before her, she clutched her son more tightly to her breast and screamed, "Murderers! You shall not have my baby!" And desperately trying to rise, she continued with a heart-rending cry, "David! Asa! Help! Help!"

Marcus, paralyzed for the moment by the shock of recognition, called to his companion, "It is Elizabeth, the wife of David!" Giving his whole attention to the prostrated young mother before him, he was finally able to convince her that he was not one of the soldiers from the palace.

"O noble Marcus, I ask your help and protection, until I am safe with David my husband," she sobbed as she related the somewhat incoherent story of her flight from the town.

The soldiers were deeply moved as they listened, and Marcus inquired, "Why is David not with you? When did you last hear from him?"

"He is not with me and his little son," Elizabeth answered tearfully. "Something dreadful must have happened to him, since he and his father left for the camp eight days ago. I fear that Caleb the Herodian has made good his promise to seek revenge."

Marcus feared as much, but said nothing. One thing was certain: He could not take the poor woman to her husband's sheep camp where she probably would find her worst fears realized. Instead, he decided to take her and the child to Leonia and leave them with her until he could find David. She needed the tender care of his wife. Bending close to her, he asked, "Are you able and strong enough to ride?"

"I have never ridden a horse, but I can try," she answered with a brave smile.

Marcus was satisfied, and turned to the silently watching Silvanus, whispering a few words to him. As the latter replied that he understood, Marcus handed the little boy to him and then assisted the frail young mother into the saddle of his mount. Climbing up behind her, he said to Silvanus, "Now let us have the baby again, and let us be gone."

Out of consideration for the poor health of the young mother, the soldiers rode at an easy pace. A half hour later Marcus drew rein before his tent and dismounted. He caught a glimpse of his wife Leonia standing between the tent flaps as he lifted Elizabeth from the saddle. The young wife of David for a moment looked bewildered around her, and seeing the row of army tents, looked inquiringly at her friends and asked, "Where have you brought me, O Marcus? This is not the camp of my husband."

"I know, my dear friend, this is not David's camp, but you can believe me that it is the safest place for you and your child at the present time. Let your mind be at rest concerning your husband, for Silvanus our friend is on his way to bring him here as soon as it is possible to do so."

The assuring voice and presence of her friend brought a feeling of comfort and security which could be seen in her tear-filled eyes as Elizabeth whispered her gratitude. But Leonia, who in the meantime had joined them, interrupted her words of thanks as she turned to her and said, "My dear, we are only too glad to give you the comfort and protection of our home, which you are so much in need of, for we have not forgotten the kindness of David and Asa. Come." And taking her gently by the hand, Leonia pushed aside the tent flaps and entered with her friend.

As Elizabeth's tired body sank into the soft fur of Persian lambskins spread over a low sleeping couch, she could not repress the sigh of relief rising from the depth of her heart. Her little son lay close beside her, satisfying his hunger at his mother's breast.

Marcus in the meantime had gone to the tent of his friend, the army doctor, seeking his advice and help for the wife of his shepherd friend. He found him sound asleep, but a reference to David roused the little surgeon from his slumber.

Elizabeth had meanwhile fallen asleep, but the fitful movements of her body told the watching Leonia that the sleep was not deep and undisturbed. Long and tenderly did she look upon the fine and lovely features of the sleeper. Then her gaze turned to little Jonathan, whose clear brown eyes seemed to study her. His tiny hands, clenched into little fists, pressed to his pink chin. The cooing child was fully contented, his small feet kicking in the soft, warm fur of the lambskins.

Leonia's child-hungry heart could not resist the temptation to take the child into her arms, to kiss the little fists as tears welled in her eyes. And she whispered softly, "Oh, for the blessedness of possessing a son like you!"

She was so deeply engrossed in fondling the child that she did not notice her husband, who had just entered the tent, accompanied by Julian. Marcus looked with loving eyes at his wife as she gazed upon the smiling child with an expression of starved maternity. The little doctor, who knew the secret sorrow of Marcus and Leonia, directed their attention to Elizabeth, who had risen with a cry of alarm to a sitting position on the couch when she noticed that Jonathan was not at her side.

Leonia, when she heard the anxious cry of her friend, rose quickly from her seat to lay the baby back into the arms of his mother and said, "Let not your heart be troubled; your son is with me. I held him but a moment in my arms. He is a sweet child, and one to gladden the heart of any woman."

Something in the tone of Leonia's voice caused Elizabeth to look up at her. "You do love my son, do you not?" she said, interpreting correctly the secret thoughts and desires of the childless woman standing by her side. The slight nod of her head and the warm glance from her wet and shining eyes told Elizabeth that she had read the woman's thoughts aright.

Marcus introduced Julian to Elizabeth, who became somewhat alarmed as she caught the scrutinizing stare of the doctor. However, when his face did not reveal the shock he sustained as he examined her, her fear was about to subside. She was quite ready, at his suggestion, to resume her slumber. But when she caught the doctor's surreptitious glance at Leonia, she refused to go to sleep. "My eyes shall not find sleep again until I have heard the voice of my husband," she cried.

A short time later the doctor left the tent with Marcus and told him the result of his diagnosis. "If we do not find her husband soon," he said, "she will not survive. The fever that consumes her will rob her of the little strength by which she has so far held on to life. The only thing that would strengthen her will to live is the sight of her husband's face."

Marcus thought of Silvanus, wishing that he would soon return, bringing David with him.

XXI

Elizabeth's Last Wish

DURING the long hours of the night, Marcus and Leonia remained at the side of their suffering friend, trying to comfort her. She was pitiful to behold, asking countless times for David, her husband. Silvanus had not yet returned, and Marcus began to fear the worst for David.

Elizabeth had once more wakened from a fitful slumber and was now looking around the large tent with feverish eyes. Little Jonathan was in her arms, sound asleep. Anguish was in her voice as she spoke. "Asa is no more. I saw him lying dead before the monster, a lance through his breast because he refused to betray the newborn King of my people. But I cannot see my beloved David, for there is such a great pain in my eyes." And as she spoke, she gently rubbed her slender hand over her burning face as if to erase the pain that was raging in her head.

Leonia did all she could to console the woman, telling her that perhaps she had had a disturbing dream. But Elizabeth shook her head and said, "Oh, do not try to tell me otherwise, for I know it was not a dream. I shall never again behold the face of my darling David." And pressing her little son to her tear-stained face, she cried, "What will become of you, my son, when I am no more?"

The two Romans were moved to tears as they listened to the agonizing lament of the woman, who had fallen back on the couch in a faint, pale and exhausted. Leonia hastened to take the child from the mother's nerveless arms, laying it down tenderly beside her.

At this moment Marcus rushed hopefully to the entrance of the tent, for he had heard the sound of a madly galloping horse coming toward the camp. However, great was his disappointment when he saw Silvanus on his lathered and dust-covered mount come to a stop before him. He was alone!

"Where is David? Why have you returned without him?" Marcus asked nervously.

Silvanus was tired and seemed to ignore the question of his friend as he listlessly handed the reins to a waiting horse-boy who led the animal away. By the sad expression in Silvanus' eyes Marcus knew that no good tidings were in store for Elizabeth. In the tent, Silvanus seated himself on a spare saddle that lay on the floor near the entrance. Leonia rose from her knees before the couch and whispered softly, "She is sleeping now, and sleep will do her good. But where is David? Did you not find him at the camp?"

Silvanus then began to tell what he had learned at the sheep camp, and what he had heard at the palace. "When I reached the place where Asa's camp formerly stood," he said, looking dejectedly at his friends, "I found to my great surprise that the camp was no more. The little mud hut lay in ashes, and the whole place was in ruins. I stepped closer, trying to find the reason for it all, and found this." With these words Silvanus pulled the broken pieces of a blood-stained sword from the folds of his tunic, handing them to Marcus for his inspection. "I came to the conclusion," Silvanus continued, "that a terrible fight had taken place at the sheep camp, and my belief in this was strengthened when I found a spot on the ground that was saturated with blood. I searched the whole place and its surroundings, but found no trace of the three herders."

After his friends had somewhat recovered from the shock

of surprise which his words had produced, Silvanus went on, "Remembering your story about the vengeful Caleb, I decided to go to the palace; and I was fortunate. Do you remember the Syrian lad whom we rescued a few years ago as he was being beaten by a band of ruffians? Well, this Jesup (that is his name), who is now a palace servant, the special valet of the treacherous Caleb, happened to be returning from an errand in the town as I was lying close by the gate. As he was about to pass by, I reached out and pulled him down beside me. He was too frightened to cry for help, but he was relieved as soon as he heard my voice and recognized me. I apologized for the abrupt manner of our meeting and immediately asked whether he could tell me something about David and Asa. Replying to my question, he then related to me fully a most horrifying scene that had taken place at the palace." Silvanus hesitated for a moment, then said slowly, "Old Asa is dead, jereeded by the hand of the maniac in yonder castle when he refused to reveal the hiding place of a certain newborn King. I am almost certain that our good friend Nathan also is dead."

They were so shocked at the terrible revelation of Silvanus that they could think of nothing else. They did not see Elizabeth as she slowly rose to a sitting position on the couch, her horror-filled eyes fixed on their backs. They thought she was asleep. Silvanus, with a heart filled with sadness, went on, "Poor David paid for his loyalty to his father and to this newborn King with his eyesight. The monster had him blinded in both eyes when he found himself thwarted in his effort to learn the herders' secret."

A cry from the bed caused them all to swing about suddenly, only to see Elizabeth sink back into the cushions, her face covered with her hands as if to shut out the horrible picture formed in her mind by the words she had just heard.

"O merciful God," she cried in anguish, "let not this be true! My beloved David blinded forever! How can he live! How can he ever behold his son!"

A painful silence fell upon the saddened friends. No one spoke. Each looked solemnly at the others, with eyes reflecting the sorrow that had now overtaken them. No one even dared speak a word of sympathy to the suffering woman, fearing it would only deepen her sorrow. At the words of the failing woman, hatred flamed anew in the hearts of the two soldiers against the scheming captain and the heartless king.

As dawn broke over the hills of Bethlehem and the first warm rays of the morning sun fell over the gray canvas tents of the Roman camp, nestling peacefully on the eastern slope of the town, Leonia and the two centurions stood watching with burning eyes the ebbing life in the fragile body of Elizabeth. For a long time she had lain as if in a stupor. But as a ray of the golden morning sun found its way through the tent flaps to her bed, she began to sit up. She looked first at the two men, then at the tear-stained face of Leonia, and spoke softly, "My friends, what I have to say to you I must say quickly, for there is but little time left to me. I am deeply indebted to you. You have all been dear friends to me in my need and distress, and I want you to know that the gratitude and blessing from a dying mother's heart will follow you in all your days to come." Stopping for a moment to catch her breath, she turned to Leonia and said, "Of you, O sweet Leonia, I wish to ask a last favor. Will you take care of my son until his father desires to take him from you?"

The hope that welled up in Leonia's heart caused the blood to rush hot to her face for a moment, for she had not given up hope that her friend would recover from her illness. "Let your heart rest in peace," she replied. "I will care for your child until you yourself are again able to do so."

But in reply the dying mother whispered with soulful appeal in her voice, "Promise me, O Leonia, that you will care for him as if he were your own. For my David will surely see him again when the two are kneeling at the feet of the Master; and I will bless you."

Leonia was so deeply moved by the plea of her friend that she could only kiss the white hand that lay on her breast. The kiss told Elizabeth that her wish was granted, and a smile of inner peace stole over her face. All the deep lines of suffering that had been engraved on the features of her waxlike face seemed to disappear. And the small hands which had been playing restlessly above the bedcover were now lying still.

Leonia's gaze never left the face of her friend. Soon the lips of the sinking woman began to move, but no sound came from them. Elizabeth's eyes were on her child, and Leonia began to understand. Without speaking, Leonia put the child into Elizabeth's arms. Only a woman could fathom the agony of the dying mother as she kissed her child for the last time.

As the pallor of death passed over the face, Leonia quickly took the baby from the nerveless fingers, calling to Marcus to bring in Julian. But the services of the doctor were no longer needed. The sorrow and suffering of Elizabeth had come to an end.

Before the sun had gone down again in the west, Marcus with the help of Silvanus and the little doctor buried the body on the little hill close to the former beloved sheep camp, where Elizabeth had enjoyed to the full the companionship and love of her beloved David.

BOOK TWO

Thirty-three Years Later

I

The Ambush

FAINT starlight pierced the deep gloom of the night, and a cool breeze began to blow from the region of the wilderness of Judea, replacing the sweltering humidity which had lasted throughout the day. A dewy moisture, settling over the valley and hills, was absorbed by the parched, thirsty earth. The caravan road, winding its dusty ribbon over mountain slopes and stretches of fertile land from the ancient city of Jericho to the olive groves of Bethany, was deserted, except for a lone rider who at the moment emerged from a dip in the road which had previously hidden him from view.

The horseman seemed to be in a hurry, his mount galloping at break-neck speed, its iron-shod hoofs raising a cloud from the dust that lay ankle-deep in the road. The rider's cloak, fastened around his neck by a silver chain with clasps, was flying in the wind, giving him the appearance of a speeding demon. The horse itself, a black stallion, blended with the darkness of the night. The soft tinkle of silver knobs and ornaments indicated that the horseman was a soldier or some person of distinction.

Onward the horseman swept, the fleet and nimble feet of his mount cutting short the distance. Not until the lights of near-by Bethany came into view did he slow his untiring mount to a light gallop. A few hundred yards ahead of him, the road wound its way through a stretch of rocky terrain, its sides covered with large boulders of limestone which were screened and surrounded by shrubs of wild ash and eucalyptus trees. This was an ideal spot for an ambush; and the horseman must have surmised as much when he viewed the place, for a look of caution could be seen in his dark eyes. Peering ahead, he noticed a taut rope stretched across the road, but before he could pull his galloping mount to a stop to avoid it, the horse went down, catapulting its rider headlong into the dust-covered road. Flinging out both arms to break the impact of the fall, he managed to save himself from serious injury.

Although the horseman could not immediately understand the cause of this untoward incident, he needed but little time to think about it, for his sharp ears caught the sound of rushing feet. "The ambushers!" he thought to himself, as he quickly wiped the white, smarting dust from his eyes. Glancing around, he saw that the dust cloud raised by his fall and scramble off the horse had settled again to the roadbed, giving him a clearer view of the critical situation which confronted him.

Still in a kneeling position, the soldier was on the alert as the attack came. The shadowy forms, clad in burnoose and head clothes, came rushing at him from the dark background of shrubbery growing close to some large rocks. Opposite him on the road was a flat-sided boulder of great size. Outnumbered as he was, he realized that the huge rock would assure him of a safe rear guard. From this protected position he would be able to give a good account of himself. Reaching the boulder, he faced the ruffians and cried mockingly, "Come, you rabble, if you are still inclined to fight, and I will give you something you will not soon forget!" His short broadsword, gripped in his strong fingers, then cut mightily through the air, making a swishing sound.

The foremost bandit hesitated for a fleeting second as he heard the challenging shout. Then throwing caution to the winds, he made a rush at the unhorsed rider. The latter could see only a pair of black, hate-filled eyes. The rest of the face was concealed by a part of the white burnoose with which the fellow's body was covered. The dagger-armed fist descended with force upon the breast of the soldier. Avoiding the needle-sharp point with a catlike movement, the soldier lunged forward, his right arm shooting toward the uncovered throat of his antagonist. With an unearthly scream the fellow dropped the dagger, flinging both hands to his bloody throat. The soldier leaped back to the protecting wall of the rock, his weapon ready for the attack of the second assassin.

The other fellow, armed with a sword, rushed wildly at the soldier in an effort to catch him off guard. In this he partly succeeded. Only through the quick co-ordination of brain and muscles, schooled in years of desert fighting, did the soldier manage to escape fatal injury. Agile as a mountain cat, he drew his body aside, but not quite far enough, for the descending sword cut an ugly gash in his left shoulder. And had it not been for the protecting cloth of his cloak, the consequence would have been serious. But, taking advantage of the favorable circumstance thus afforded him, he drove home his own weapon.

The burly bandit, in order to place himself in a better position to deliver a fatal blow, approached his victim warily and then made a deadly lunge. But before he could lift his weapon a second time, the cavalryman struck with lightning speed, and the fellow went down before him with a terrified cry. He tried to regain his footing, but his ebbing strength failed him, for the wound he had received was mortal. The soldier's weapon had gone through the ruffian's back, leaving him dead at the feet of the victorious horseman.

The soldier stood for a while staring down at his last victim, and a feeling of dizziness almost overcame him. Mastering this feeling by sheer power of his will, he began to study his frightening situation. He could not understand the reason for the murderous attack, for he knew of no enemies that would seek his life.

Bending down, he uncovered the face of his slain assailant and eyed it with curiosity. It was a face strange to him. By the cut of its features he concluded that he was looking at a Jew. So engrossed was he in studying the face that he was for the moment unmindful of his surroundings. He did not see the blur of a fleeting shadow as it glided ghostlike from boulder to boulder on his left. Nor did he see it emerge from behind a clump of bushes and step into the road behind him.

Too late did he become aware of the new danger. Not until he felt the hot breath of a bandit on the back of his neck did he realize that he had not disposed of all of them. No time was given him to meet this new foe face to face, for the descending weapon of the bandit quickly buried itself in the back of the horseman, and as his body crumpled in a heap, he heard the curse of the brigand, "Die, dog of a Roman!" as it came mockingly to his ears.

Bending over his victim, the assassin pulled the dagger from the motionless form, wiped it clean on the soldier's garment, and gazed at the bodies of his fallen companions, meanwhile murmuring a curse under his breath. "Fools, you paid with your lives for not listening to me. In your eyes I was a coward. You could not see the wisdom of my words of caution, and your scheme has brought you nought but death!"

Turning away from the bodies, the bandit looked at the soldier's stallion with covetous eyes. He tried to seize the trailing reins, but gave up the attempt as the horse kept shying farther and farther away from him. And by the feeble light of the moon, he went through the garments of the soldier, searching for some valuable loot; but all he found was the dagger and sword of the Roman. Hiding these trophies in the folds of his clothing, he turned his back on the ghastly scene, and a moment later he disappeared into the darkness of the night.

The Good Samaritan

QUIET now prevailed, and silence hovered over the still forms lying in the road. No sound was heard except an occasional tinkle from a silver knob that ornamented the headstall of the lone stallion, which had remained faithfully at the side of his fallen master. The moon had risen high, throwing its pale light over the scene. The hungry cry of a mountain lion came floating over the distant slopes of Jericho, causing a pair of wild hares to scurry for a near-by cover.

After the assassin had departed, the stallion continued to nibble on the grass that grew along the edge of the road. An hour later he trotted back to the side of his master, and his fine little ears shot forward as he saw the figure begin to stir. The right arm of the rider, whose body lay prone on the ground, began to move.

Slowly it rose, only to fall weakly into the dust. The sound of pain from the blood-covered lips of the fallen rider brought the stallion closer. Trying to arouse his master, the stallion nudged him with his velvety muzzle, and gripping the cloth of the cloak with his powerful teeth, he began to pull gently at it. Again the rider made an effort to rise, but with a groan he sank back to the ground. The stallion then pulled more vigorously at the cloak, but his effort was futile. Then he sent a loud whinny into the moonlit night, his head standing erect, his eyes shining as he looked expectantly up at a ridge a few hundred yards away.

A lone traveler was coming over the crest of the hill.

Though supported by a staff, he had the walk of a strong man. His head, covered with a wide-brimmed hat, sat on a body built like that of a giant. An old threadbare mantle hung over a pair of broad shoulders. The cool night wind played around his bearded face, out of which peered a pair of mild blue eyes, overshadowed by bushy eyebrows which blended with the snow-white hair that fell to his shoulders. His loins were covered with a piece of linen cloth over which was girded a fleecy lambskin. He wore the customary sandals of the country, fastened to hard-muscled calves by soft leather thongs.

At the sight of the riderless horse standing in the road, the lone traveler came to a stop a few feet from the nervous animal, eyeing the scene before him with surprise and curiosity. In front of him lay the body of a Roman soldier, face down in the dust, his brass-burnished helmet marking him as an officer. A few steps farther, at his left, were sprawled two more bodies. His gaze lingered for a moment on their faces, coming to rest on an object that hung by a small silver chain from the neck of one of the fellows. Bending over the dead man, he removed the object by simply breaking the chain.

Looking at the small round metal disk as it lay in the hollow of his toil-worn hands, he murmured, "Zealots!" On one side of the disk could be seen the rough outline of a lion's head, while the other side was covered with an inscription which the old man was unable to decipher. A look of sadness crept into his mild blue eyes as he dropped the disk back upon the breast of the owner. Turning slowly away, he murmured softly, "The Lion of Judea! What a mockery! Used as a cover for the evil instinct and killing lust of robbers and assassins!" The old man, a Jew, knew very well of this Jewish secret political organization which sought to break the

Roman yoke over his people by terrorizing the land with its killings and robberies of Roman soldiers and officers.

As his keen mind began to reconstruct the scene before him, the traveler looked up and took some notice of his surroundings. When he did so, he found the empty scabbard of the soldier, which indicated to him that one had survived the struggle, for he could find no trace of the Roman's sword. Perhaps, he conjectured, it had been taken as loot by the survivor. The stallion, standing with pointed ears and uplifted head a few yards away from him, suggested the presence of some one in the vicinity.

Suddenly his eyes opened wide. He noticed a slight movement of the soldier's out-flung arms. Throwing his staff upon the ground, he knelt quickly beside the prostrate form. Turning the body over with a pair of strong but gentle hands, he raised it to a sitting position, using one of his knees as a back rest for it. With one free hand he loosened a tooled leather wine flask from his own girdle, pulling out the stopper with his teeth. Pressing the flask to the bloody lips, he began to feed the wine slowly, drop by drop, into the parched mouth of the wounded man until he noticed a slight tinge creep into the waxlike face. Placing the stopper into the mouth of the flask, he laid it beside him on the ground. Next he took the old, threadbare plaid from his own shoulders, rolled it up on his bent knee and, placing it in proper position, lowered the head gently upon it. Then he proceeded to probe for the wound that had left blood stains on his hands.

After a close examination he discovered the wound in the soldiers back and was startled at the sight of it. Speaking aloud to himself, he said, "It's no wonder that this poor man has sunk into a faint! It is a miracle that there is still some life left in him!" Looking for a long moment into the pale features, he gave further expression to his thoughts, "He will yet be a dead man if he does not at once receive the services of a doctor. But how I am to obtain such help for him, I surely do not know."

As if in answer to his perplexity, the stallion began to neigh. The herder's eyes lit up as he glanced at the proud animal and said gently, "Perhaps there is yet some way to obtain help for your master; and you, my friend, may be chosen for the task."

Speaking gently to the horse, the herder managed to grasp the trailing reins and secure the horse by tying it to a low-hanging branch of an oak a few feet from the road. Wrapping the still unconscious man in the old mantle, he laid him with tender care across the saddle. He himself walked along by the side of the horse.

Gray dawn was beginning to appear in the east as he pulled the stallion to a halt before a small cottage built of white sandstone. The house sat well back from the rough village road and was bordered in front by a well-kept flower garden.

Fastening the reins to the lattice of a rose arbor that formed the entrance to the garden, the old man hastened to the door. Instead of knocking, he reached up to the door lintel and pulled on a leather cord which allowed the door to swing wide open. Returning to the waiting horse, he lifted the quiet form from the saddle with the tenderness of a mother, and with it started for the cottage.

A pair of young and frightened eyes greeted him as he stepped over the threshold with the burden in his arms. "Rebecca, my child," the old man said, "hasten and bring a light." The young girl seemed not to have heard her father's words, for her horror-stricken eyes were watching the blood-less face of the soldier. "Come, come, my daughter," the old man spoke more urgently, "do not linger, for haste is needed!"

Turning her eyes from the waxlike face, the girl then rushed ahead, lighting an oil lamp that stood on a window sill of the small room into which her father was following her. In a corner stood a hand-hewn bed, covered with homespun blankets and skins of lamb. Laying his burden gently down upon it, the old man turned again to his daughter and said, "Child, I need your help. Light a fire and heat some water, and bring me some pieces of linen." Pity and sympathy were reflected in the girl's eyes as she clung to the arm of the old man. "Is he dead? Oh, how dreadful! How did it happen?" she asked excitedly.

"No, my child," the old man replied softly, guiding her gently to the door, "he is not dead. But he will be soon if we delay any longer in obtaining help for him."

III

Jason and His Daughter

THE old man watched his daughter as she left the room, his eyes filled with a father's pride. His name was Jason. He was the owner of many flocks of sheep that roamed the plains and hills of Bethany and Jericho. In the town and surrounding country he had a reputation as a man possessing the gift of healing by methods known to no one but himself. Though nearly sixty years of age, he was still a man of great strength. His generous heart and countless deeds of charity made him one of the most highly esteemed men of the town of Bethany.

As the herder looked for a long time down into the pallid face of the wounded man, a slight shudder passed through his body. Shaking his head in bewilderment, his bearded lips moving, he uttered incoherent sentences. "Merciful God, what do I see! Or is this a dream! This would be too great, too wonderful to be true, after all these years of patient waiting!"

Strong emotion gripped the old herder as he continued to study the wounded man. His eyes beheld a fine face with well-formed nose and mouth. And despite the loss of blood, the tightly closed lips marked the man as one of great power of will. A high, smooth forehead was crowned with a shock of raven-black hair, cut short at the base of a strong-muscled neck in compliance with the rule of the Roman army. His hands, burnt brown by the desert sun, were slender but manly. His muscular limbs and broad chest gave proof of the great strength he had before the murderer's steel laid him low.

Jason had just finished removing the cloak in which he had wrapped the soldier when his daughter returned with the water and linen. He took the pitcher and poured some of the water into a small wooden basin which Rebecca had brought from the kitchen. Carrying it over to the bed, he set it down beside him and began to examine the wound more carefully.

A startled cry of pity as well as horror broke from the lips of the girl when she saw the ugly wound exposed before their eyes. But the old man disregarded her agitation, since his entire attention was concerned with cleansing the wound of the grime and dust that had become embedded in it, at the same time praying that his treatment would not cause a renewal of the bleeding. He then rose from his knees and walked over to get a small cedar box that stood on a small shelf above the door. The soldier had so far shown no sign of returning consciousness; but as Jason poured into his open mouth a few drops of liquid from a small phial which he had taken from the box, he nodded with satisfaction when he noticed a favorable reaction.

Rebecca anxiously watched the gentle hands of her father as he worked patiently over the soldier, and her young and tender heart prayed for the best. "O father," she whispered, "he is beginning to revive!"

Jason smilingly agreed without pausing in his ministrations. After he had finished dressing the wound, he laid the man on his right side so that the injured back would be free from pressure. Then for the rest of the night they waited hopefully, but it was not until the first rays of the morning sun shone through the colored window panes of the room that they could see the result of their untiring effort. The black-browed eyes began to open and to stare aimlessly at the wall and ceiling of the dimly lighted room. Seeing this, the girl rushed to the bedside and, laying her soft white hand gently on the forehead of the young man, looked up with an expression of deep anxiety.

Her father sat on the little wooden bench near the door, his chin buried in the hollow of his right hand, reading correctly the anxious thoughts of his daughter. "I know, my child," he said, "he is burning with fever, and I am helpless, for I can do little more to subdue it. We must depend on his youth and trust to the mercy of the Lord Almighty."

Rebecca, still looking down at the man, noticed suddenly that his lips began to move. Bending over him in the hope of catching some softly whispered words, her face turned red as his dark brown eyes seemed to beg her not to leave him. Jason knelt down quickly beside his daughter, anxious to hear whatever words the young man might be able to speak. But he was too late to hear anything, for a terrible spasm of pain shook the soldier's body, and a trickle of blood appeared at the corners of his mouth.

Shocked at this sudden turn for the worse, the herder looked with alarm into the eyes of the soldier. A picture flashed before his mind, and his lips formed a name, but his thought remained unspoken. The sight of the blood on the wounded man's lips caused him to cry out to the frightened girl, "Quickly, Rebecca, get me some cushions!"

Hastily she left the room and returned at once with cushions from her own bed. With the utmost tenderness Jason began to prop up the half-conscious man to a sitting position, supporting him with the pillows which his daughter had brought.

Seating himself at the edge of the bed, Jason after some effort managed to force the soldier to swallow some wine. Though somewhat encouraged by this success, he was still greatly distressed, and he expressed his concern to his daughter, saying, "What am I to do if this man should die? Perhaps I have too readily burdened myself with another man's troubles. I would fare none too well if I should be found with a dead Roman on my hands. I wish he would rally at least to such an extent that we might learn his name and destination."

Sooner than he had expected, he was relieved of his anxiety. The stimulating wine had had its effect. Slowly the tired eyelids began to lift, and the soldier, regaining consciousness despite his intense pain, asked slowly, "Where am I, and how did I get here?"

"My heart indeed rejoices at the sound of your voice, O stranger," Jason replied softly, "for now I may be able to secure for you the help you are so badly in need of. You are in the humble dwelling of Jason, a herder of Bethany. I found you lying in the road, the victim of an assassin's dagger. At first I thought you dead like the other two men whom I saw lying near you in the dust. But I soon discovered that there was still a spark of life left in you. I had no other choice but to bring you here into my own house, for you were in need of immediate help."

As Rebecca came to the bedside to join her father, the latter ceased speaking and, taking the girl's hand, smiled at the young man and said, "This is my daughter Rebecca." Rebecca responded with an attractive blush.

A slight tinge likewise colored the face of the Roman as he whispered softly, "You are indeed a blessed man to be able to call this girl your own." The old man and his daughter could see the effort it cost him to talk. Yet he would not heed their advice to lie quiet for a while. "I thank you for your kind words," he continued, "but I am a very sick man. I fear I have but little time to spare. My name is Dara, and I am the son of Marcus, a centurion of the Roman Horse Guard at Jerusalem. And I pray you, my friend, send at once for my father if it is possible for you to do so."

As Dara spoke, the herder's face was a mixed expression of pleasure and perplexity. "Marcus of the Horse Guard!" he murmured to himself somewhat absent-mindedly. But the soldier's question, "Do you know my father?" brought him quickly back to the present as he replied with slight hesitancy, "No—no, I do not know him, but I have heard of him."

Rebecca, who had listened quietly to the two men, felt uneasy as she observed the sad look in her parent's eyes. She had seen such a look on his face only once before, and that was when at the top of a hill near Bethlehem they had rested for a while on their journey to the Holy City. But out of respect to his feelings she had never dared ask the cause of it.

Jason rose and whispered a few words to his daughter, who, nodding, left the room at once. He then turned to the soldier and said, "Be assured, O Roman, I will go in haste, and I myself will try to secure for you the help of your parent." The girl returned at this moment, carrying a steaming bowl of soup in her hands. With a gracious gesture the herder continued, "It would please me if you would drink of this strengthening broth which my daughter has prepared for you."

The girl did not wait for a response from the soldier, for she had already seated herself on the edge of the bed, lifting the bowl gently to Dara's lips. Just as Jason was about to leave the room in preparation for his journey to Jerusalem, he was stopped by the young man's feeble "Wait!" and as he returned to the bed, the soldier handed him a small ivory locket that hung on a little silver chain around his neck, the only article of value that had escaped the greedy eye of the ambusher. "Take this, my friend," he said feebly. "It will

help you to gain immediate speech with my father, if you
will show it to the guard. Try to reach my father at a time
when my mother is not present. I want to spare her the
shock which the sad news of my condition will surely
occasion her."

A gleam in the herder's eyes reflected his respect for the
wounded man as he heard these tender words. Hiding the
little round locket in the small leather pouch hanging from
his girdle, he smiled tenderly, "It shall be done as you desire."

Pressing a warm kiss on the smooth forehead of his daughter, he left the room and soon afterwards was on his way to
find Marcus in Jerusalem.

I V

Marcus and Julian

THE black stallion of the wounded Roman soldier, grazing behind the house, raised his head and looked at the herder as he came through the back door. At the sight of the beautiful animal, Jason for a moment thought of using it for his trip, but soon rejected the thought and said to himself, "No, I shall fare better without him, for some curious people might wonder at seeing a poor herder astride so grand a steed."

Little clouds of dust, whirling up in the wake of his hurrying feet, testified to the herder's urgent haste to reach his destination. No thought of stopping to rest entered his mind as he hurried along the dusty road, and at intervals he talked aloud to himself, mentioning the name of the man he was asked to seek and to bring back to the cottage. "I wonder if it really is the Marcus, the friend of years ago."

The mild blue eyes of the aging herder swept over the countryside that stretched out in full view before him. Memories of days gone were vividly recalled. But the slight droop of the broad shoulders indicated that not all those days were free from toil and care.

The sun was high in the sky as he entered the city through the sheep gate, pursuing his way unerringly through the crowds of peddlers, beggars, and market criers who were plying their respective trades in the narrow streets of the ancient city. Paying but slight attention to the noisy life of the bazaars and the shops of the merchants, and glancing indifferently over the stately mansions of wealthy citizens, partially hidden from the eyes of the teeming crowds by high walls, Jason hurried on until he came in sight of the old Fortress Antonia, better known to the people as the Hill of Zion. This fortress, known at one time as Fort Baris, was used by Herod as an armed camp and was a small city in itself. It housed the Roman garrison and provided living quarters for the officers and their families.

The sentry on guard looked with raised eyebrows at the poorly clad herder as he approached the gate. Ribald laughter rang from the deep, narrow windows of the guardhouse as the old man began to address the soldier. The guard, with feet planted wide and solid on the cobblestone pavement, gripping the hickory shaft of his spear with his right hand, his left forearm slipping through the broad leather bands of a bronze-coated buckler, leered mockingly at the Jew. "So!" the sentry jeered. "So you would like to have speech with the noble Marcus! And what could this business be that brought you here so early? Will you tell me that, O son of a stinking woolly!"

The herder's mighty hands closed into a pair of formidable fists at this biting taunt. The guard, however, failed to notice the menacing gesture. But soon Jason so controlled himself as to be able to answer the arrogant soldier. "Your words, O Roman," he shouted to the startled sentry, "prove that you are indeed no better than a braying ass! You are cursed with ignorance as well as bad manners! I asked you with due respect for permission to see the centurion Marcus, but an insult to my person was your only response."

Both men were so deeply absorbed in their altercation that neither of them noticed the approach of an old soldier whose tunic and dress marked him as an officer. The quiet but strong voice of the newcomer broke in upon them as he addressed the sentry, "What is all the quarreling about,

Sallust? What does this man wish?"

The sentry, trying as best he could to suppress his anger as he saluted his superior, said rather heatedly, "This dog of a sheepherder wishes to have speech with you, O noble Marcus; but he would not divulge the reason for wishing to see you. I therefore denied him entrance."

The eyes of the centurion for a moment looked searchingly at the Jew, then turned back to the scowling sentry. "If this man's business is with me, it is not for you to decide whether or not he shall see me," Marcus said sharply.

The sentry stood motionless at the rebuke, offering no excuse for his haughty words to the herder. Then the officer, addressing Jason, asked courteously, "What is it, my good man, you wish to see me about?" Jason had no ready answer, for his mind, as he looked into the eyes of the soldier, was occupied with only one thought: "Beyond all doubt, this is Marcus, the friend of David and Asa."

Somewhat annoyed at the herder's silence, the soldier repeated his question, and he was surprised when Jason asked in reply, "Are you the Centurion Marcus of the Roman Horse Guard?"

As their eyes met for a moment, the soldier felt that the old herder was no stranger to him. Perhaps the notion was absurd, but further consideration of certain rather vague recollections seemed only to strengthen it. Aware of the watchful eye of the sentry, he hesitated slightly but finally answered, "Yes, I am he. How can I be of service to you?" Without direct reply, Jason brought forth the ivory locket of Dara and, handing it to the puzzled centurion, said with much feeling, "Do you recognize this?"

With an expression of recognition and genuine surprise, the Roman examined the medallion lying in the hollow of his hand. Dara's talisman! A look of suspicion shone in his heavy-browed eyes as he looked searchingly at the herder again and asked excitedly, "How did you come into possession of this locket? Where is my son Dara?"

Jason then related his story and concluded with the remark, "If you wish to see him still alive, I advise you to make haste and bring a doctor with you.

The warning was hardly given before Marcus was on his way to the stable, calling back to Jason to wait for him. A few minutes later he returned, leading two horses. By his side strode a little man who tried unsuccessfully to keep pace with the hurrying soldier. Marcus introduced him as the Doctor Julian. The herder looked for a fleeting moment at the humorous face of the little man, then swung quickly up behind him on the back of the capering mount.

Jason was the first out of the saddle as they reached the little cottage soon afterwards. The two Romans were close at his heels as he hurried up the garden path toward the house. The door opened slowly, and in its frame appeared the sweet face of Rebecca. When the two soldiers showed too plainly their admiration at sight of her virgin beauty, Jason found a convenient pretext for sending the embarrassed girl on an errand to a neighbor's home, and then with a motion of his hand he bade the soldiers follow him.

Filled with disturbing emotions, Marcus looked at the fever-flushed face of his son. The little army surgeon at first hesitated to disturb the sick man, but he knew that further delay would be serious. Accordingly, drawing Marcus gently aside, he asked for hot water and dressing material, and as he began to examine the wound, he said, "I need more room here; the tunic must come off."

Jason, standing at the foot of the bed, offered to help and slowly pulled the blood-crusted garment over the head of Dara. Laying it down at the foot of the bed, he glanced over the doctor's shoulder at the exposed wound. When he did so, his face turned ashen at the sight of the birthmark between the shoulder blades of the young man. It was a star the size of a man's fingernail!

Marcus, noticing the change of color in the herder's face, was startled at the old man's whispered words: "The star of —little Jonathan!" The words seemed to linger for a long time over the group at the bedside as if to intensify their significance.

The little doctor, still occupied with the dressing of the wound, looked up into the disturbed face of the old Jew. As he felt the deathlike silence occasioned by the latter's softly whispered words, he asked, "What is it, my friend; are you ill?"

"Nay, nay," Jason answered quickly, "I am well, but tired, for little sleep has blessed my eyes since I left Jericho two days ago."

Despite the herder's reply, Marcus could not dispel the feeling that this was not the whole truth, but just now he had no way of assuring himself.

Julian the Curious

A SHORT while later Julian completed the dressing of the wound and with the assistance of Jason and Marcus laid the patient in as comfortable a position as the wound would permit. Washing his hands in a small wooden basin, he informed Marcus of the result of his diagnosis and said, "He might survive, Marcus, if the fever does not sap too much of his strength. The boy must not be moved from here for a long while. He needs care and quiet, and that means that he must have the care and help of Leonia."

Jason, still standing at the foot of the bed, felt the eyes of the Romans centering on him, and, raising his head, he said with a pleased look, "Consider my humble dwelling as your own, O Marcus, and I shall feel honored."

Deeply moved by the generous offer, Marcus stepped to the side of the old herder and said, "The darkness of my sorrow is brightened by the comforting words from your noble heart. I shall never forget them. What you have done for my son will be forever gratefully remembered, and I hope you will accept this small gift as a token of my gratitude." With this remark the centurion pressed a small bag of money into the hands of Jason.

But the herder's fingers did not close around the bag, and it fell to the flagstone-covered floor with a heavy thump. Over Jason's face rushed a trace of red as he looked into the startled eyes of the soldier and said, "Why do you spoil the beautiful words from your noble heart with the sordid gift

of money? What I have done for your son I have done out
of compassion. I would not do less even for a wild animal
that was in need of my help. For how shall we expect mercy
from the Lord if we have no heart for His creatures?" And
without waiting for a reply he excused himself and left the
room.

Too disconcerted to speak, Marcus stood in awkward
silence. Then Julian, aware of his friend's embarrassment,
stepped to his side and said, "Live and learn, my friend.
What a peculiar fellow! In spite of all his trouble—sacrificing
sleep and rest for the sake of your son—he still acts strangely
toward you. Why? Perhaps," the little doctor went on,
"perhaps the old man is right. There *are* things which cannot
be paid for with gold. What he has done, he has done in a
way that gives me the highest respect for his character."
Stopping for a moment to feel Dara's pulse, he turned to
Marcus again and continued, "What puzzles me is the way
the old fellow looked at Dara. I cannot overcome the feeling
that the two are not strangers to each other. Perhaps I am
wrong in saying this, but that is the way I feel about it.
There seems to be some secret in the fellow's past which he
is making every effort to conceal."

Had not the situation been so serious, Marcus would have
laughed at the words of his friend. He had known the little
surgeon a long time, and he knew also of his persistent trait
which sometimes had proved very unpleasant to him. When
the fellow's curiosity was once aroused, he would never rest
until the matter before him was settled to his complete
satisfaction.

Though Julian was of small stature, there was in his round
bald head a keen and active mind. His large blue eyes could
take on a frosty stare when he was annoyed, but they could
just as readily express warm sympathy when he encountered

suffering and misery. His friendly smile revealed a set of perfect white teeth that gave his somewhat homely face a winsome and trustful expression.

Despite the fact that Marcus had full confidence in the little man, he hesitated to disclose to him his own thoughts regarding Jason, for he had not yet recovered his composure. But he was aware of the doctor's questioning stare and said to him, "Julian, my friend, I see your curiosity is working harder than ever. True, I realize now it was a tactless way to show my gratitude to the good old man. But, I ask you, would you have done otherwise? I also must admit that there is something noble in the man's character; but as to your suspicion that the two men are not strangers to each other, I say that you are wrong and that your imagination is playing you some trick."

The hot temper of the little surgeon flared up as he listened to his friend's criticism, and snapped back heatedly, "So you think I am dreaming again and imagining something that is not true. But hearken to me, how do you explain the strange behavior of the good fellow when he saw your son's birthmark? And do not tell me that you do not know of what I am speaking, for I observed you both!"

Marcus was about to fly into a rage, but he controlled himself and said with a surprising calm, "There are some things in life which are much better left unmentioned. So let us forget the matter and go see how the boy is getting along." Julian, though inclined to prolong the argument, reluctantly subsided and said no more as they tiptoed to Dara's bedside.

An uneasy silence hung over the room as the two men listened to the labored breathing of the young man. It was an absorbing picture to see the two old soldiers—men accustomed and hardened as they were to seeing death and bloodshed—hovering over the wounded man, their eyes filled with an expression of pity and anxiety.

After an absence that seemed hours too long, Jason returned, carrying a tray piled high with fruit. As Marcus reached for some of this, he looked earnestly into the eyes of the herder and said, "My friend, do not hold against me my awkward way of showing my gratitude to you for your unselfish service to my son. I am greatly ashamed of it."

Jason, conscious of the soldier's sincerity, replied warmly, "There is in my heart no bitter feeling against you, O Marcus, for to err is only human, especially when one's pride is hurt."

A gentle knock sounded, and through the opened door Rebecca came into the room and stood beside Jason, who with fatherly pride in his eyes presented "My daughter Rebecca."

Marcus glanced admiringly at the lovely girl and bowed low before her. The doctor, who was equally impressed with her beauty, said, "A beautiful flower hidden from the rays of the sun!" In Rebecca's long-lashed hazel eyes he saw a deep mountain lake surrounded by a grove of dark pine trees. A row of pearly white teeth glistened through a pair of soft, warm lips, and a mass of glossy black hair was caught up in a perfect coil at the back of her graceful neck.

Sympathy and anxiety for the stricken young man could be read in the perfectly molded features of the girl's oval face. Her presence was a soothing balm to the raw, strained nerves of Marcus as he kept watching her while she changed the cold compresses on the fevered forehead of his son. Softly and tenderly the feminine fingers moved over the flushed face of the sick man; and this always seemed to give him new strength and to buoy up his hope for recovery. And as the shadows of eventide darkened the small window of the sick room, her cheerful services were, she felt, amply rewarded by the young man whose lingering gaze into her eyes expressed something more than mere sincere appreciation.

Marcus, almost overcome with emotion at his son's evident improvement, was extremely eager to ply the boy with questions. But Julian objected to this, for he did not want the young man to become excited, and ordered absolute quiet for him. Dara, however, did inquire after his mother and asked whether she had heard of his misfortune, and when Marcus ventured to tell him of the doctor's suggestion that his mother be brought to the cottage to take care of him, a smile of satisfaction lighted his peaceful face.

Dara having taken some nourishment and then fallen asleep, Marcus and Julian made ready to return to Jerusalem to call for Leonia. Julian would have preferred to stay longer at the cottage, but a strong sense of duty told him that his services were required at the fortress. After giving Jason instructions for Dara's treatment, Julian joined Marcus at the door, where both spoke their farewells. At a brisk gallop they were on their way to Jerusalem.

NIGHT had fallen, and quiet hovered over the streets of the ancient city of Jerusalem as they approached the gate of Antonia. Throwing the reins of their mounts into the hands of the stableboy, they separated, each going to his own quarters. Marcus walked with a heavy step, for he had not the courage to tell his wife the disturbing thoughts that occupied his mind.

Leonia met him at the door. On her face was a questioning smile as she looked up at him and inquired, "Where have you been, my dear, all the day long?"

A feeling of anxiety was apparent in her voice. Marcus, to gain more time, avoided a direct answer by telling her that he had been called away on some important matter. But he was not accustomed to keep anything from his wife, and his face showed that he was not telling her the whole truth. Her soft lips were waiting for the kiss which did not come at once. For a moment there was silence. Then she led him into the comfortable living room and questioned him further. "Now, dear Marcus," she said, "tell me who it is this time who needs the help and services of Julian. Do not attempt to evade my question. I saw Julian return with you."

He looked at the still beautiful face, framed in wavy black hair with a sprinkle of gray, giving the small face an expression of tender, sweet womanhood. She was clothed in a flowing garment of the finest linen, held at the waist by a girdle of scarlet silk.

Marcus was reluctant to bring sorrow to his wife, but he

had no other choice. Slowly he handed her Dara's locket. Bewildered, she took it from his hands and looked at him, her fear-filled face searching his. Then he told her the story so far as he knew it, however being careful not to cause undue alarm, and then concluded by saying, "As soon as you are ready, I will take you to him."

Leonia did not utter a cry as she pressed the small ivory disk to her trembling lips, and the terrible fears which had agitated her mind subsided somewhat when she saw the brave smile on her husband's face. "I will be ready at once," she said.

She entered the adjoining room and presently returned with a heavy wool plaid, which Marcus gently put around her shoulders, and a few minutes later they were on their way to Jason's house.

Rebecca, aware of their arrival when she heard them stop before the rose arbor, opened the door to light their way into the house. And as Leonia stepped over the threshold on the arm of Marcus, she met the shy but respectful gaze of the young girl and was struck at the sight of her beauty. Gently she stretched forth a hand and said softly, "My sweet child, you do certainly deserve the name of Rebecca. You are indeed a creature of enchanting beauty." And throwing an arm around her shoulders, she said, "May I kiss you?"

To hide her emotion, the young girl led the way to the sick room, where they found Dara awake. His whispered greeting to his mother was drowned in the stifled sob of the woman as she sank slowly down at the bedside. No words were needed between the two to tell of their affection for each other.

Rebecca in her quiet, gentle manner did much to disperse the gloomy silence that hung for a moment over them all. She left the room and returned with hot broth, which Leonia began to give to her son. Marcus and Jason were seated on the little bench that stood by the door, each occupied with his own thoughts. Dara, too weak to continue talking, lay with closed eyes, his haggard face betraying the pain he was suffering.

Marcus remained as long as possible with the others at the bedside, but as midnight approached, he could not longer delay his return to Jerusalem. After a gesture of farewell to the rest, he said to Leonia, "I am sorry, my dear, for being compelled to leave you, but I am on duty tonight at the fortress. Our host and sweet Rebecca will be a help and comfort to you here."

Marcus left the cottage, and, although he had but little time to spare, he rode at an easy pace, for his mind was preoccupied with the person of old Jason. He could not explain his interest in the man—who he was, and where, if ever, he had seen him before. Unconsciously the soldier began to express his thoughts aloud. "If I did not know that my friend of long ago was dead, I should be tempted to think that this was he. But he is dead, killed at the sheep camp, and I have the word of Jesup, the Syrian, for it. Still it is true, we never found his body."

These thoughts were interrupted as the horse came to a stop before the mighty gate of the fortress. A tall, shadowy form detached itself from the dark wall of the guardhouse as Marcus slid, weary and tired, from the back of his mount; and a voice filled with anxiety called out to him, "Marcus, where is Dara?"

"Silvanus, my friend, is it really you?" the centurion cried excitedly as he recognized his old friend.

Silvanus, though pleased to see Marcus again, was too much concerned about Dara to talk of other matters. Brushing aside his friend's effusive welcome, he repeated his question, "Where is Dara?" Marcus then took his comrade by the arm and, leading him past the wondering sentry, whispered audibly, "Come to my quarters, and I will tell you."

VII

Leonia and Rebecca

AFTER her husband's departure, Leonia was alone with her son, for Jason and his daughter had left the room. Her heart was heavy and her eyes hot from unshed tears. She busied herself trying to reduce the fever in the pain-wracked body of her son as she applied cool and soothing compresses to his head. To her mind came a scene, a scene she had lived over and over when she thought the life of her son was in danger. The place of that scene was not far from where she was at present.

At the memory of it, a sob escaped her lips as she whispered, "O Elizabeth, my dear, surely this cannot be the end of all my dreams. He cannot die, for your promise has not been fulfilled as yet. David has not yet asked for him." Tears trickled down her cheeks and fell unnoticed upon the restless hand of the sleeper.

All her woe and misery were manifested in the words of anguish which she uttered as she fell upon her knees before the bed, not knowing that she was praying, praying to a God unknown to her. She knew only that if destiny had willed it, Dara, her son, also would have been praying to this God whom Elizabeth called Almighty God. Her heart and soul yearned for relief in the supplicating cry, "O Thou unknown God of my soul, in the memory of Elizabeth, I am here before Thee. Spare the life of my son, and I will believe in Thy power and in Thy name until my dying hour."

She was not aware that Rebecca had returned to the room and was a witness to her agony and prayer. It was only after her tears had ceased and a feeling of peace had come into her troubled heart that she noticed the girl standing at the door. Her face became scarlet as she rose from her knees. Rebecca, knowing what had taken place, shyly put an arm around Leonia's shoulders and said softly, with a glance at the bed, "Your son, O lady, is blessed indeed in having a mother like you, so good and sweet."

Leonia, comforted by the girl's sweet utterances, took her gently by the hand, leading her to a little footstool close beside her, and smiled into her face, "It is sweet of you, my child, to speak thus. Dara is indeed as noble a son as a mother could wish to have."

The smiling eyes of Rebecca, lingering on the pale features of the sleeper, told the woman much of what went on behind the lovely forehead of the young girl. A slight ache pulsed through Leonia's breast, but nothing in her voice betrayed her feeling as she asked the girl to tell her more about herself. Rebecca, glad for an excuse to remain longer in the room, moved a little closer to the woman and, taking her gently by the hand, said, "There is little to tell, dear lady. I am the only child of my father. He reared and cared for me ever since I can remember. My mother died when I was two years of age." And, as if she had just remembered something of great importance, she rose from her seat and said, "Come, dear lady, with your kind permission I should like to show you something."

Rebecca, still holding her by the hand, led her over to the small deep-set window of the room. Opening it slowly, the girl pointed with a slim hand toward the star-filled sky and breathed with a slight tremor in her voice, "Sweet lady, did you ever gaze at the stars at night when they shone in all their heavenly beauty, and did you ever, with your heart and soul filled with the wonder and greatness which your eyes behold, ask yourself by whose power this mighty universe came into being?"

The Roman woman shook her head slowly and whispered, still at a loss as to the meaning of the girl's words, "No, I have not. I have always taken the existence of such things for granted, a gift to us mortals from the gods. But now," she continued hesitatingly, "as I look into your sweet and innocent face, and listen to the earnestness of your soul, I feel that I must lack some knowledge, and I would thank you if you would tell me more of the great power of which you are conscious."

"Gladly will I do this if you will but have patience with me." The girl's face brightened from inner joy as she began to speak of the difference between the Roman gods and the worship of her own people. "You Romans believe in many gods," Rebecca said, "whom you serve at many temples. These gods are made by the hands of men, pretentiously displayed in places of splendor and wealth. To them you bring gifts and offerings according to the favors you expect from them. And never does it occur to you that these gods are only things without life. Man can give only form to the things he makes. He cannot give life. Only the God of my people is able to do that. He is an invisible God. There are no other Gods besides Him. He is merciful and ever faithful, and He will hearken to any supplicating cry that rises from a true heart."

The girl paused for a moment, gazing into the star-filled sky. Leonia, standing by her side, looked with rapture into her sweet face and whispered, "Do not stop, O child; but tell me more, that I might understand."

"Forgive me if I assume too much," Rebecca went on. "I do not know to whom you prayed a short while ago. I know only that my heart is bleeding for you as it feels your grief, and is longing to be of help to you. I feel this God of my people is a God unknown to you. Perhaps you have never heard of Him. Despite all this, He is your only hope and the only source from which your son can receive lasting help."

"The only source and hope for my Dara!" the woman repeated, more to herself than to the girl. She walked away from the window to sit at the edge of the bed, looking down at her son, and said, with hope and joy in her voice, "For your sake, I will believe in this God."

A shuffling sound caused the two women to look toward the door, where they saw the old herder come into the room. He smiled inquiringly at them. The moist eyes of Leonia indicated to him that there had been no improvement in the boy's condition. His eyes, filled with sympathy and pity, shifted for a moment toward the bed, then he turned to Leonia and said with feeling, "Let not despair find rest in your heart, sweet lady. For when sorrow seems the greatest, the mercy of the Lord is nearest." Then, after a slight pause, he continued, "If you will permit me, I will gladly watch over your son for the remainder of the night, and my daughter will prepare a place in which you may rest."

Leonia, touched by these kind words, replied, "I thank you, noble friend, for your kind offer, but it is not I who am in need of rest, but you yourself."

Nodding respectfully, he ceased speaking and left a few moments later with Rebecca, who was longing to tell her father of the conversation she had had with Leonia, but she decided not to do so at this time.

Dawn broke over the gray ridges that surrounded Bethany as Jason rose from the pallet on which he had slept and went to the yard behind the house to care for the black stallion. The two had become friends, and with loving hands the herder began to groom the horse. Now and then Jason looked

along the ancient caravan road that ran its course through
the town. At the sound of rapidly approaching horses, Jason
stopped brushing and rushed to the front of the house.
Three horsemen had already dismounted before the rose
arbor.

He recognized Marcus and Julian, but the third man was
a stranger to him. Marcus came slowly up the garden path,
greeting Jason with a warm handclasp, introducing to him
the stranger as an old friend of his family. A pair of keen
brown eyes under bushy eyebrows held the herder for a
moment and at first occasioned him some embarrassment.
But with a courteous nod to the stranger, he welcomed the
trio and preceded them into the house.

They found a tired but happily smiling Leonia as they
entered the small room, and joy shone in her face as she
saw the tall, imposing figure of Silvanus entering behind
her husband. Rising quickly from the little footstool beside
the bed, she pressed with warmth the extended hand of the
soldier and said, "Silvanus, my friend, I am glad you have
come." Then, overcome with emotion, she leaned for a
moment against the soldier, crying softly. The others in the
room hid their own feelings as they saw the soldier who,
with a look of sympathy, pressed her small head against his
breast and said tenderly, "Do not despair, O Leonia, and have
hope, for the darkest hour is that just before the dawn ushers
in the sweetness of the morning." And, as if to shake off his
own turbulent thoughts, he stepped to the bedside, looking
down into the haggard face of the young man, and said, "If
he had only waited for me, this might not have happened."

Then the soldier began to relate the circumstances leading
up to Dara's misfortune. "Dara and I had been sent to
deliver an important message from our superior officer at
Carthage to the Roman Procurator at Jerusalem," Silvanus

began. "On reaching Damascus, I was forced to interrupt my journey for a few days because of urgent business that awaited me there. But Dara, too impatient to wait for me, decided to go on without me so as to return to you without delay. And I, to my sorrow, allowed him to go.

"It took more time to finish my business than I had anticipated, and when I reached Antonia a few hours ago, I was told by the guard that Dara had not arrived. Nor could I find any of you at home. By chance I encountered Sallust while I was looking for you. It was he who first intimated that something was wrong. But all I could do was wait, for Sallust did not know where you had gone."

A short time after the soldier had stopped speaking, Dara awakened from a restful sleep and looked into the brown eyes of Silvanus, who was standing beside the bed. He smiled pleasantly and said, "I am glad to see you again, Silvanus, sound and whole before me. As for me, rashness and impatience have brought but poor reward."

The little doctor forbade further conversation and heartened Leonia with the words, "He will recover, for the fever has already abated."

Rebecca, with a pitcher of water in her hands, had stepped quietly beside Julian, who, moving back from the bed, looked with admiration at the blushing girl and said in cheerful tone, "If he does not get well when tended with such beauty and devotion, he deserves only misery!"

The deep blush on the sick man's face betrayed his affection for the girl, who was now refreshing him with the cool water. All except the doctor looked on with joy in their hearts. His experienced eyes did not miss the budding of their young love and wondered how it would end. To himself he said, "And I must be the bearer of the sad news that will shatter their bright dreams." At present only the doctor suspected how serious Dara's condition really was.

Time wore on as they sat quietly talking. Leonia had stepped to the window to cool her heavy eyes and soon afterwards seated herself beside her husband on the little wooden bench by the door, listening, half asleep, to the conversation of the three men.

When Rebecca and her father were not present to hear them, the men were talking about Jason, and it was Silvanus who began by saying, "I have seen the fellow before, but where, I do not know."

The doctor's face brightened with expectancy as he leaned toward the speaker, and Marcus, seeing this, suppressed a smile. He knew that Julian was about to burst forth again. And he did, for as Silvanus was pointing out the peculiar behavior of the herder when he had thanked him for his service to Dara, the little fellow spoke up, "I will tell you why he is acting this way: He is afraid of something; but of what I do not know."

Wiping the top of his shiny, hairless head with a small silken cloth and noticing the smiling faces of his two friends, he continued with fervor, "Very well, you may laugh, but hearken to my word and give me an answer to this: Why did he deny us an answer when we asked him whether he had ever lived in Bethlehem? He had only to answer yes or no. Then I would have been satisfied. But he refused to commit himself. There is something he is withholding from us, something he fears may come to light."

Silvanus had not paid much attention to what Julian was saying, for his observing eyes had noticed an object that stood on the shelf above the door. Rising from his seat, he walked over to the door and removed from the shelf a small medicine box. Studying it for a while, he turned around and placed it into the lap of Marcus, who looked at it for a moment, then said, somewhat bewildered, "What is the meaning of this?"

An excited look shone in Silvanus' face as he asked, "Do you not recognize this box?"

Marcus shook his head slowly and said, "No." He then looked at Silvanus for some explanation.

"Very well, open it; then let your memory serve you," Silvanus replied, somewhat annoyed at his friend's slowness of thought. "Who saved your life and cared for you? And who cleansed your wounds and sores, and bound them with soothing balm when you lay near death in the road near Bethlehem?"

Silvanus could say no more, for the astonished Marcus cried out excitedly, "Asa's cedar box! But by the great Pollus, how did it ever come into the hands of our good host?"

"That I do not know, my friend," Silvanus answered. "But we can find out. Let us call in the herder, and we shall probably find the answers to our questions."

VIII

Waiting for Jason's Story

J ULIAN had already left the room in search of Jason and soon afterwards returned with him. The herder was quick to note the tension in their faces as he glanced at them, and asked the reason for his being called into the house. For an answer Marcus handed him the little box and asked, "Does this box belong to you, my friend?"

"Yes," the herder answered. Then hesitating a moment, he said, "Yes, it belongs to me. But why do you ask?"

Silvanus watched the herder closely and detected a perturbed look in his face. Then, having found a satisfactory approach to the problem of establishing Jason's identity, he said, "Good Jason, we are greatly indebted to you. And I ask your pardon if I seem rude in telling you that you have not told us the whole truth concerning this box."

Jason turned an angry red at the soldier's rather direct suggestion and said peevishly, "Who will gainsay my claiming it as my own?"

"I will," Silvanus smiled. "And I will prove my words to you. Listen to the story I have to tell you. Many years ago a Roman soldier, homeward bound, fell into an ambush on the road near Bethlehem and was left as dead by the ruffians. But he did not die, for he was found alive by two young herders who were on their way home to their camp. The two men carried him to their camp and cared for him. The camp was owned by the father of one of the young herders. And it was he who really performed wonders in saving the Roman from certain death. They became devoted friends, but soon thereafter they were parted forever by the hands of a mad king and his satanic tool, a captain of his household guard."

For a moment the soldier was silent, meanwhile eyeing the old man closely. Then he continued, "Before their friend, the Roman, could come to their rescue, the old herder had died a horrible death at the fortress, and his only son was blinded for life. The other young man fared no better, for a band of Thracians slew him as he resisted them at the camp, which they completely destroyed by fire. We know that this little box was in the hut and should have burned with it. But it was not destroyed, otherwise it would not be here. We know there does not exist another one like it. The old herder himself made it. This is my story." The soldier ended and, looking directly at old Jason, added, "It remains only for you to tell us the names of these unfortunate herders."

Marcus, who had listened intently to the story of Silvanus, thought it absurd to see anything definitely significant in Jason's possession of the box, and said, "How could our friend here know these men, for of a certainty he was not acquainted with them?"

Before Silvanus could answer, Jason said, "I thank you, O Marcus, for your trust in me. But Silvanus has spoken the truth. I do know the names of those herders. For many, many years I have whispered their names over and over whenever my memory recalled their tragic fate. For these names were once love and life to me."

For a moment he shut his eyes, as if to recover from the strain of his confession. Then, as his eyes slowly opened, he looked intently at Leonia, who had fallen asleep with her head nestling on the shoulder of her husband. Marcus was puzzled at Jason's revelation and, coming closer to him, said, "You speak in riddles, my friend, which I find it difficult to understand."

Jason then turned to the soldier and replied, "Do you not yet know me, O Marcus? Do you not recognize in me the friend whose death you have mourned all these years? I thought my secret safe and securely hidden from all the world. But the Lord has willed it otherwise. It was the observing eye and keen memory of your friend that identified me."

Julian had not missed a single word, and his large eyes beamed with satisfaction when he heard Jason's reference to him. His suspicion, which he had so many times voiced to his two incredulous friends, was now being justified. Leonia, who had awakened while Jason spoke, had caught the last words of the herder. All those present, except Silvanus, looked with astonishment at Marcus, who, rising from his seat, stretched out his arms toward Jason and cried, "By the gods, of a truth I must have been blind not to have recognized you before this!"

Warmly clasping Jason's hands in his own, he gazed into the old man's face with overwhelming joy and said, "I can hardly yet trust my eyes when I look at you, O Nathan—alive before me! But why, my good friend," Marcus asked, "did you not confide in us and let us know that you were still alive?"

The old herder, seeing the joyful expression in Marcus' face, was not able to answer at once. He looked into the happy faces for a long while, then at length said quietly, "Have patience, my dear friends. Gladly will I tell you all you want to know. But first of all, grant me this favor, that nothing of what I have to say to you will be repeated to my daughter Rebecca until such time as you find it necessary for her to know it." The request was cheerfully granted. Thereupon Jason promised to resume his story after his return from the near-by village, where he had some unannounced business to attend to.

Julian was a most miserable man just now, for he was obliged to return to Jerusalem within an hour or so and would thus be deprived of the opportunity to hear Jason's story at first hand. But before he left, the little doctor with some show of triumph at having been right thus far, challenged his friends to hazard a guess at the essential facts of Jason's promised denouement.

Silvanus, ever ready to ruffle the temper of his little friend, said with an impish grin on his face, "My good Julian, perhaps you have forgotten the old proverb which says that even a blind hen can find a grain of wheat—sometimes!"

Marcus was amused as he noticed the rising anger of the doctor who, already astride his horse, was reproaching himself for his own stupidity in seeking justification of his suspicions about the old herder. Silvanus, eager for a final thrust of raillery, looked at his peppery friend and said, "Forget not, O Julian, to put this gift of yours to work, and perhaps you will find the answer to Jason's secret and silence even before you reach the gates of Antonia!" A cloud of dust, raised by the swirling hoofs of the little man's spirited mount, was his only reply.

Marcus and Silvanus, for want of something more interesting to do while awaiting Jason's return, went to the rear of the cottage, where their mounts were grazing, and seated themselves on a small sandstone slab, their thoughts still filled with the developments of the last few hours. "What a revelation!" Marcus exclaimed. "Nathan alive all these years, when we thought him dead! But all this makes me think of Dara. What about him, Silvanus? Do you think Jason knows whose son he really is? And what shall we do about it?"

Silvanus looked sharply at his friend for a moment and, with a tone of confidence in his voice, said, "What are you in fear of? How is the boy any concern of Jason? Jason is not the boy's father. Dara, in a way, belongs to me as much as he does to you and Leonia. And do not think for a moment that I would give him up to become a sheepherder. No, not after all my years of struggle and care to make a soldier of him. Remember," Silvanus continued, in justification of his words, "no crime was committed in obtaining possession of him. Nor was coercion used to bring him into the family, for he was given to Leonia to be cared for until such time as David should claim him again. And that, my friend, will never happen, for David is dead, for all we know."

Marcus still did not feel at ease concerning the situation despite the well-reasoned assurance of his friend and indicated as much when he said, "How, my friend, shall I explain Dara's birthmark to Jason? For I am certain that he recognized it."

"Do not explain anything to him!" answered Silvanus, somewhat annoyed at his companion's persistent fears. "If he should ask anything about it, just put him off for the time being with evasive replies; and keep Leonia informed of your plan. It will be a matter of only a few more days when the boy will be strong enough to be taken to his own quarters in Jerusalem. Then all your fears will be at an end."

IX

Jason's Story

WHEN Jason returned in the early evening, he found Silvanus, Marcus, and Leonia waiting for him in the largest room of the house, which served its owner at times as living room, dining room, and reception room. His friends plainly indicated their tense eagerness to hear the story of Jason, who was equally anxious to continue the account which he had interrupted several hours before. In reply to his inquiry regarding the whereabouts of Rebecca, his friends informed him that she had left on an errand which would keep her safely absent for at least another hour. Thus assured that his daughter would not overhear him, he began, "Friends, what I have to tell you is perhaps not unknown to you, except possibly the manner in which I escaped and managed to live. Ever since the tragic event of more than thirty years ago I have been living in constant fear of being apprehended for the murder of big Bardia. For the law would call it murder. But never, not for one moment, did it enter my mind to kill the fellow; I merely wanted to disable him. But as he slipped lifeless from my arms, I had no time to regret the folly of my deed, for the other Thracians attacked with redoubled fury.

"With the sword of big Bardia, which I managed to snatch up from the ground, I gave a good account of myself. But there were too many of the ruffians, and I was forced back to the door of the burning hut. Suddenly, when I heard the shrill whistle of my friends, I turned my head for but an instant to shout a warning to them. At that moment the murderous steel of a Thracian, who had come upon me from behind, was thrust into my back. I continued fighting for a while, but my strength left me suddenly, and I knew no more.

"How long I lay thus, I do not know; but when I regained consciousness, I found myself lying in a pool of blood before the fire-gutted hut. Too weak to rise and tortured by thirst, I began to look around, expecting to see the bodies of David and Asa. But they were nowhere to be seen. My despair, however, was relieved somewhat by this fact, when on second thought I reflected that perhaps they had somehow managed to escape capture.

"Morning was not far off, but the bone-chilling air and the heavy dew caused me to shiver with discomfort. Suddenly I heard a slight noise on my right, and, as I turned my head, I saw the familiar face of an old man whom Asa had once befriended. I knew him as Isaac, a trader from near-by Jericho. He had been on his way to the town with a load of merchandise and had seen the last dying flames of the camp as he was still some distance away. Removing the bundle of wares from the back of his donkey and hiding them under some bushes, he managed in some way to put me upon the back of the patient animal and brought me to his own home in Jericho.

"My recovery from the dreadful wound was due to the untiring care of Rachel, the only daughter of my benefactor. As soon as I was able to talk, I told Isaac of the terrible tragedy and asked him to find out, if possible, what had happened to Asa and David. The next day he returned with the disheartening word that he could find no trace of them. I was naturally distressed at this, and I urged him to continue his search for my friends.

"Willingly he complied with my request and left the house once more. A few days later he returned, and at first he seemed to avoid me. I thought I knew the reason why, and this did little to improve my condition. But soon afterwards he told me the result of his latest search. He said that so far as he was able to learn, Asa and David, even Elizabeth and little Jonathan, had disappeared, and that no one seemed to know what had happened to any of them. He told me also of Herod's cruel 'Slaughter of the Innocents' at Bethlehem.

"This news, instead of completely disheartening me, gave me new strength and courage, for there then surged up within me the determination to become well and strong again, so that I myself could go out in search of my missing friends. But almost two months elapsed before I was able to do this. And it was a task fraught with much danger, for I felt that I was regarded as a murderer. True, Caleb thought me dead. But there remained always the possibility of my being apprehended by some of the authorities.

"Countless times I went to our former camp with the hope of discovering some trace of my friends. But my efforts here were fruitless. What I really should have done was to go to Bethlehem. Too late did I remember Lea, the neighbor of Elizabeth. A long time afterwards, when I finally went to Lea's home, I was told that she had died. Her friends knew little more than I did concerning David's wife and little son. The only encouraging information I received was the assurance of the neighbors that little Jonathan had not been found by the mercenaries as they ransacked David's home. He probably is alive.

"My friend, the trader, had managed to bring the scattered sheep of Asa over to the hills of Jericho, where they were cared for by one of his trusted servants, giving me the assurance that the inheritance of David's little son was safe and secure.

"By mere chance I learned what had happened to my

friends. I was returning from Jerusalem, where I had gone in search of them, when I fell in with a peddler going to Bethlehem. In the course of our conversation he told me of his trading at the Fortress Antonia in Jerusalem. It was difficult for me to conceal my excitement when he said, 'That cruel monster Herod is surely on the rampage again. It was a sad affair—the one about the two sheepherders whom he ordered to be arrested. The rumor is that they knew about a certain newborn King, but refused to betray Him. In a mad fit of rage, provoked by the iron-willed refusal of the two men to give up their secret, he slew the older man with a jereed hurled by his own hand. The younger man fared but little better. When he refused even under torture to speak, they blinded him for life.'

"The peddler never knew of the agony and despair that surged through my soul as I listened to his words. I was relieved when the town came into sight, where our ways parted.

"Back in Jericho, I related all this to Isaac and Rachel. Now knowing the worst, we planned revenge. Many were the plans by which we hoped to snare the wily Captain Caleb, to force from him some information concerning the fate of David, so that we at least might learn whether or not he was still alive. And I never gave up the hope of finding him some day.

"Countless nights did I lie in ambush in the neighborhood of the castle, waiting for a glimpse of the fiend. But all this was in vain, for Herod died soon afterwards. With his death my last hope fled, for Caleb, fearing retribution at the hand of Salome, the king's sister, disappeared from the Fortress and was never seen again.

"Rachel became my wife, and we settled here in Bethany, for I wanted to be away from everything that reminded me of those dark hours of my life. Five years later Rebecca was born. While she was still a little baby, her mother died. I gathered courage to live, but only for the sake of my child and with the faint hope in my heart that some day I might meet David again. Isaac, my wife's father, died a few years ago, leaving his riches to my child, thus assuring her of a life of comfort even after I have passed away.

"As for myself, I am still a poor herder who guards and seeks to preserve the inheritance of little Jonathan, whom I have never mourned as dead, despite the fact that no one has ever seen him or his poor mother since that fateful day."

Every eye in the room was moist when the old man ended his story. Leonia's tear-filled eyes looked with pity at Jason as she said to him, "Gentle host, your suffering has been great, and we all feel with you and share your sorrow, and if you will permit me, I will tell you of a dream I had when I fell asleep this afternoon on my husband's shoulder."

Marcus and Silvanus looked expectantly into her shining eyes as she continued, "I dreamed that as I was weeping over the body of my wounded son, a voice said to me, 'Cry no more, O Leonia, and wipe away your tears, for he, whom you call son, will live to behold the face of his father. And just as I awoke, I heard you confess your rightful name, and I was not surprised, because Rebecca has taught me to have faith and hope in the mercy of the Almighty."

The faces of the three men showed deep perplexity when they heard these words from the woman's lips. Marcus was speechless. And the suspicion that Jason knew who Dara was troubled him anew, as the herder now looked at the sleeping Dara and whispered with trembling lips, "The Lord is more merciful to me than I deserve in permitting me to behold once more the son of my beloved friend David."

Then Jason, as if unaware of the presence of the others,

fell on his knees before the bed and bowed his head in prayer. Marcus was meanwhile greatly troubled to know whether further disclosures would oblige him and Leonia to forfeit Dara as their son.

As Jason rose from his knees, he asked Leonia to complete for him the part of the story about Elizabeth and her child. Leonia told him in simple words about the flight, death, and last wish of Elizabeth, and added with feeling, "We buried her at the deserted camp of Asa, the only spot where we knew she would have wished to be buried. We never told Dara, for we thought it best for him not to know of the terrible tragedy of his loved ones. We did not harm anyone by so doing, for Asa, his grandfather, was dead. You too were thought dead, for no one knew of your miraculous escape. And poor David was never heard of again.

"But the sudden and unexpected revelation of your identity has thrown a different light on the affair. Not that it affects in any way my relationship to Dara." The woman breathed heavily as she glanced at the quietly listening herder and continued, "Dara is my son and shall remain my son so long as I can draw a breath. Elizabeth gave him into my care. She knew that I loved him. Even his real mother could not have loved him more. He means everything to me. When his rightful father shall claim him from my hands, then and only then will I give him up!"

The two soldiers breathed a sigh of relief at Leonia's firm declaration, and they waited with bated breath for Jason's answer. After a moment's silent consideration of Leonia's statement, he replied, "Dear lady, I have heard your desire, and I will respect it, despite the conviction that David, his father, would not want him to be a Roman soldier. For he was born a Jew, and he will rejoice when he learns of his Jewish origin."

Approaching footsteps on the garden path told of Rebecca's return from the town and caused them to cease their conversation. Jason rose from his seat as the girl entered the room and excused himself, for he had chores to do. Leonia, taking Rebecca by the hand, entered with her into Dara's room. They found him awake. His mother went softly to him, felt his pulse and forehead, and, finding the fever on the wane, said, "O Dara, I feared greatly for your life. But now I behold with joy that you are much better, justifying my trust in the Lord." Then, noting the questioning look in his eyes, she corrected herself, "I mean . . . thanks to the timely help of Jason and sweet Rebecca," glancing at the girl, "you are on the road to recovery."

Marcus, upon hearing his wife's expression, wondered about her corrected remark, but said nothing about it and soon afterwards left the room to seek Silvanus. He found the latter seated beside the old herder on a large stone bench in front of the cottage. Slowly he sat down beside them and listened to their conversation. They had been talking about the possibility of David's still being alive, and Marcus, reading their thoughts, encouraged their belief when he said, "I am convinced that David is still alive, for, you see, the monster of the castle died only a short time after the 'Slaughter of the Innocents' at Bethlehem, and furthermore, the death of David was never confirmed.

"But," Marcus continued, "looking at the matter in this way, I mean—supposing he had still been alive at Herod's death, why did he not return home? For we know that after the tyrant's death every prisoner that had lain in his dungeons had been set at liberty if he was not proved to be a prisoner of quality and importance. And certainly David was not classed as one of these, being only a blinded sheepherder."

Marcus ceased speaking for a while, then, eyeing the

herder closely, he went on, "But this is beside the point. What we should have done, after Caleb disappeared, is never to have ceased in our search for him. I can not shake off the feeling that in finding Caleb, we would find David."

Silvanus and Jason did not respond to this remark at once, for Marcus had voiced their opinion. For a long time nothing more was said. Their eyes swept over the town, over the carefully kept gardens and groves of silver-leafed olive trees, overshadowing the flat-roofed housetops simmering in the hot noonday sun. From the interior of the little house came the gentle voice of Leonia talking to Rebecca. As they rose from their seats, Jason turned to Marcus and said, "Your words, O Marcus, are the echo of my heart, and they have renewed the hope in me that some day I shall hear of this fellow Caleb." And the herder's malletlike fists rose for a moment as he exclaimed, "May the Lord have mercy on him, for *I* shall have none!"

Night approached as they were all asked to partake of the frugal evening meal, served to them by Jason and Rebecca. After they had finished, Marcus, rising from the table, turned to his wife and said, "I am sorry, my dear, but I must leave you now in the care of Silvanus, for on the morrow I must leave for Caesarea by the order of the Procurator. I shall return in the course of a week or two." When he saw the tears in her eyes and the anxiety written in her worried face, he threw an arm around her shoulders and said reassuringly, "I shall not tarry on the way, and friend Silvanus and our kind host will be a comfort to you."

Both went to Dara's room and looked for a while at the quietly sleeping man, whose even breath told them that the crisis had passed. Soon afterwards, Marcus mounted the waiting Adallo, Dara's beautiful black stallion, and rode away. Leonia, in the doorway, listened to the strong hoofbeats for some moments after horse and rider disappeared into the darkness of the night.

X

The Inn of the Gladiator

A FEW days later Marcus reached the old seaport of
Caesarea in the early hours of the evening. His
face and riding gear were coated with a thin layer
of dust. Adallo had fared no better. His glossy
black coat was travel-stained and sweaty, but no trace of
weariness could be seen in the proud lift of his head as they
made their way through the streets teeming with peddlers,
bronze-skinned slaves trundling pushcarts, artisans shouting
their wares, and the other sights and sounds of a busy port
city. Many in the crowd looked with admiring eyes at the
horse and its rider. Marcus' eyes swept over the wide expanse
of the harbor as he rode along the old coast road and called
to mind the man who was responsible for the great shipping
facilities of the old seaport.

"Herod of a certainty knew how to spend the people's
money. But," Marcus mused as he looked at the large, imposing fleet of ships anchored close to the shore, "when one sees
this masterpiece of engineering, one must admit that he
spent it very wisely—at times."

Herod, with his love for engineering and architectural
design, had expended large sums to improve and beautify
the city. He was especially proud of Caesarea's port facilities,
which could readily accommodate even the largest man-
of-war.

Entering the boulevards of the colonnades where the
nobility and scholars held their daily rendezvous and where
public affairs or the latest gossip about some outstanding

favorite of Caesar or Herod were discussed, Marcus, impressed by the many magnificent heathen temples, remarked to himself, "Herod certainly spared no expense to win the good will of Caesar!"

The sunset was reflected in a purple haze from the face of the harbor as he pulled Adallo to a halt before a low sandstone structure that stood at the end of a narrow street.

Over the entrance, nailed to a wooden beam, was a sign with a picture and the inscription: "Inn of the Gladiator," better known to its customers as Romar's inn. At the sight of the flat-roofed building with its weather-beaten sign and low, time-seasoned entrance of red oak, Marcus was pleasantly thrilled at the prospect of meeting his innkeeper friend.

Dismounting, he led the animal over to stand by the door, the only free spot where he could secure his mount, since the rest of the rack was occupied by a number of dozing horses, standing hipshot.

As Marcus entered the inn, the men in the low-ceilinged room took only passing notice of him. Two bronze-skinned Syrians, leaning with elbows on the edge of a table, were intently watching a quartet of fellows who were occupied with a game of dice.

The proprietor of the inn, a short, stocky fellow whose broad shoulders indicated unusual strength and whose face was disfigured by the scars of a swordsman, looked searchingly for a moment into the soldier's face. Marcus, still standing near the door, smiled in recognition at sight of the former gladiator, and Romar at the same moment leaped up from the empty wine keg that served him as a seat, and came forward with outstretched hand to welcome the soldier. "By the jaws of Cerberus," he exclaimed, "if it is not my old friend Marcus!" Marcus warmly grasped the proffered hand and replied, "Blessed is this day in which my eyes once more behold my loyal friend!"

Hearing the exchange of enthusiastic greetings, the gamblers and the two Syrians looked questioningly at the strong and stalwart figure of the Roman as he went with the innkeeper into a little back room which served as office and storeroom. A rude cot, which stood in the corner, and a round table made of oak, together with three sturdy straight chairs, made up the furnishings of the semi-dark room. A few wine kegs stood along the wall. Romar reached up and opened a small, shuttered window through which the last fading rays of the sinking sun came into the room.

"That is better," he said, smiling at Marcus. "I keep it closed during the day, when I enjoy a little nap, especially when old Sol is too oppressive." Marcus understood and smiled his response.

A servile attitude and doglike devotion were evident in every action of the old gladiator as he continued, "You are travel-weary, my friend, and you must have come a long way, judging by the appearance of your garment. So permit me to serve you. First, we shall have a drink together, then I will tell Nadia of your arrival. She will see to your comfort."

He left for a moment and returned with a large beaker of wine. The soldier took the cup from his hands and said warmly, "I pledge this cup to the welfare of my host and his sweet daughter, for I am fortunate in having a friend like you, O Romar."

Embarrassed, the fellow turned about and went back to the public room. Marcus looked toward the door, through which the burly figure of Romar had vanished, and whispered to himself, "Good old Romar, rough, yet of gentle disposition."

His mind then went back to the day when they had first met. Romar, a former gladiator, was in his youth the toast and joy of the followers of the arenas in Rome, Corinth, and

Antioch. He enjoyed this distinction until he was ambushed by a quartet of men who blamed him for the death of their brother, whom he had defeated in open and fair encounter He probably would have lost his life had it not been for the timely arrival of Marcus and Silvanus, who rescued him.

Romar was a sorry sight after the struggle came to an end. Bleeding from the many wounds he had received, he was taken by the soldiers to their quarters, where Julian, their doctor friend, used all his medical skill to save the poor fellow's life. Romar was obliged thereafter to give up his hazardous trade, and he therefore had no certain means of livelihood. He became a very unhappy man as he faced hunger and misery, for he had saved but little of the spoils of his former triumphs.

It was Marcus who, taking a liking to the unfortunate fellow, suggested to him the idea of opening a hostelry, saying to him, "You have many friends who, I am sure, will always stand by you."

Soon thereafter, the former idol of the arenas found himself installed as the proud proprietor of the "Inn of the Gladiator." Romar's inquiry as to who had financed the undertaking always remained unanswered. But he had a good idea as to the one who was responsible for the successful undertaking.

Marcus and Romar were sometimes separated for years at a time, but whenever by chance Marcus happened to visit the seaport, he did not fail to call on his old friend.

Another Old Acquaintance

MARCUS had just finished washing his face and hands when he heard the angry bellow of Romar's voice from the barroom. A few moments later there came to his ears a cry of distress that caused him to open the door to learn the cause of the commotion.

He found Romar bending over the form of a man who was trying to ward off a blow from the innkeeper's fist. When Romar, his fist still poised in the air, noticed that Marcus was about to interfere, he hesitated to strike the fellow, rather venting his anger in an outburst of cursing. "Dog of an Idumean, have you so soon forgotten the beating from my hand at our last meeting! Or has your contemptible master sent you here for another serving?"

"No—no!" the wretched man pleaded. "Do not pommel me again, for I am too old to endure it; I have not come here at my master's order, nor does he know of it."

His curiosity aroused, Marcus stepped calmly to the side of the innkeeper and said, "Friend Romar, it would please me if you would give the fellow a chance to explain his reason for coming to your inn."

Without a word, Romar relaxed his iron grip on the man's shoulder and, glancing at the speaker, replied, "You are right, Marcus. But my anger overcame me when I found this wretch here, despite my warning to him to stay away."

In the meantime the man had risen to his feet and stood looking at Marcus, who was deeply moved by the wretched appearance and forlorn expression of the miserable fellow.

Moved by pity, he decided to learn more about the fellow and smiled encouragingly, "My good man, fear not the wrath of Romar, for he of a certainty will listen to what you have to say."

For reasons best known to himself, Romar pointed to the small private room and growled, "Let us go in there, so that we shall not have a dozen ears to fill with something that concerns them not."

Passing the four dice players and the scowling Syrians at the table, the three of them entered Romar's private room, and as the door closed behind them, the innkeeper said rather sullenly, "Stop your trembling and sit down, and let us hear what you have to say." Before the fellow could make a reply, Marcus asked, "Tell me, my good man, who are you, and what is your name?"

Before replying, the old man eyed Marcus for a moment, as if to guess the soldier's reason for the question. But all he could read in the rugged features of the Roman was kindness, a kindness which he had seldom known. "Good sir," he finally stammered, "perhaps it will please you to know that I am very grateful for your timely help. I am but a poor servant, and kindness was ever a stranger to me, for I have experienced but little of it in all the days of my misspent life. And as to my name, I am called Jesup, the Syrian, and am known as the servant of Obed, the horse trader."

When the fellow uttered these simple words, Marcus experienced a shock of great surprise. Almost overturning the table as he suddenly rose from his chair, he leaned forward eagerly to study the features of the equally surprised Syrian. The name Jesup instantly evoked a flood of memories and revived an almost forgotten purpose.

Was it possible that this poorly dressed man before him

was Jesup, the friend of Asa and David? But why, he asked himself, was he in such poor circumstances? He, the former servant of the once mighty Idumean Caleb! His face paled for a moment when he suddenly remembered Romar's heated shout in the barroom, "Dog of an Idumean!" What could he have meant by that? Did he not know that the fellow was a Syrian? There could be only one explanation. Turning for a moment to Romar, he said with a sigh of gratitude, "You do not know, O Romar, what service you have rendered me today when you in your anger cursed this unfortunate fellow!"

But the innkeeper, who did not catch the meaning of the soldier's remark, silently followed the conversation of the two men with increasing interest. Marcus looked across the table directly into the eyes of Jesup and asked, "Jesup, do you know who I am?"

The fellow shook his head and answered with some hesitancy, "I am not privileged to know your name."

"I believe you," Marcus nodded, "but when you say that your master's name is Obed, you do not speak the truth. For I happen to know him by another name, a name most bitterly hated by all the people of Judea!"

Realizing that any denial in the face of Marcus' full certainty would be futile, Jesup with a blush of embarrassment acknowledged that the soldier was right. Marcus continued, "I had given up hope of ever finding a trace of this man. But my hope is now renewed, for you, my friend, will lead me to him." Seeing the consternation in the fellow's eyes, Marcus ended assuringly, "Fear not, Jesup. No harm will come to you, for I am your old friend Marcus of long ago."

Romar, entirely ignorant of the meaning of all this, broke his silence by repeating his former question to the fellow, "Why did you disregard my warning, knowing the consequences if you should be caught in here again?"

"It was the sight of a horse," Jesup answered, "which even now stands before the inn, that gave me the courage to enter. I wanted to make the acquaintance of its owner, to inquire whether he would be willing to sell the animal. My master is desirous of information of this kind, and he throws a few denarii my way as a reward for it."

"And that will impoverish him but little," Romar retorted grimly, "for does he not reap a goodly profit through your services?"

At this moment Nadia, the innkeeper's daughter, appeared in the doorway, carrying a tray filled with dishes of food for the soldier. At sight of her, the Syrian seemed to shrink into the shadow of the small room, but her penetrating glance spied him quickly. Her face began to grow pale as she looked at her father for an explanation. "Fear not, my child," Romar quickly reassured her, "this man is not what we thought him to be, for our friend Marcus calls him his friend. I have done him a great wrong, and it would please me if you would shake his hand."

Hesitating a moment, the girl complied with her father's wish and began to set the table for the soldier.

Jesup, feeling somewhat more at ease at the sudden change of tone on the part of Romar and his daughter, expressed the desire to leave, offering as an excuse that his master would be displeased if he were to remain longer. Marcus, however, would not accede to this request, but called Jesup back to the table and said, "Be seated, my friend, and our host will refresh you in mind and body with a cup of wine from his own favorite keg, while I ask a few questions of you concerning your master."

Romar left the small room, while Nadia picked up the empty tray and returned to her own living quarters, which

were situated in a small room to the rear. Romar returned
a short while later with a jug of wine and two ornamented
silver cups. After filling the cups to the brim, he politely left
the room, leaving the two men alone with their problems.

For a while neither of them spoke. Marcus, occupied with
his dinner, which he found to be delicious, studied the Syrian
as he stared into his half-empty wine cup and looked at him
with a feeling of compassion as he said, "Tell me, Jesup,
something about yourself, and perhaps I might be able to
help you."

The Syrian, touched by the generous offer and hopeful of
possible release from the life he had been forced to lead
these past thirty years or more, began to unfold to the listening centurion the story of his flight from Antonia after the
death of Herod, how the wily captain at the point of a
dagger had prevented him from leaving his service. "He promised me great riches and an independent future," he added,
"and what other choice had I but to follow him? For I was in
his power, and I still am. I no longer have any will of my own. I
have at times been obliged to lose my self-respect in doing for
him under compulsion the many things I have done."

Down his haggard face a tear trickled as he unfolded a
picture of years of misery and of mistreatment at the hands
of the Idumean. Having heard Jesup's sorry tale to its conclusion, Marcus rose from his seat, walked around the table
to lay a gentle hand on the shoulder of the speaker and said,
"Say no more, my friend, but rest assured that before the
sun sinks low in the west again, you shall be a free man, if
you are but willing to do as I shall bid you."

A look of hope filled the Syrian's eyes as he heard the
Roman's promise, and a world of joy opened up before him
as he whispered, "Oh, to be free once more and to be a
man again!"

XII

Cornelius of the Italian Band

G ENTLY but firmly refusing to permit the disappointed
Romar to accompany him to the impending meeting with the horse trader, Marcus, mounted on
Adallo, once more shook the hand of the innkeeper. Thanking him for his hospitality, he rode off in the
direction of the upper city.

A short time later he pulled rein before the gate of a large
mansion. The sight of a gong, which resembled a buckler,
hanging from an iron rod above the ornamented gate, assured
him that he had reached his destination.

Dismounting slowly, he stepped over to the shield, took
a wooden mallet from the gate, and struck the gong three
sharp blows. Before the deep-toned waves of the gong had
subsided, a figure loomed out of the night. It was a servant
carrying a lighted torch. By its illumination, which dispelled
the darkness from around the gate, the servant saw the horse
and its rider. Recognizing the familiar uniform of a Roman
officer, he gazed respectfully at Marcus and said, "Enter, sir,
in the name of God. I will inform my gracious master of your
arrival." And then, while speaking, he swung open the iron
gate to admit the visitor.

Closing the gate behind them, the servant courteously led
the way to the stables. As Marcus walked behind him, he
said to himself, "Something tells me that my friend Cornelius
has changed his way of living, for he now employs servants
with the manners and speech of gentle folk."

A brown-skinned stableboy appeared, offering to take

care of Adallo; but Marcus politely declined the offer and said, "I myself prefer to see that he is cared for." Lest his remark be mistaken for rudeness, Marcus gave the young fellow a silver coin.

A broad path, strewn with white gravel, took them to a spacious stable, where the stallion was greeted with soft neighs from a score of saddle horses as they scented his presence. Knowing that Adallo was in good hands, Marcus left him soon afterwards and followed the torch-bearing servant to the house.

Passing softly murmuring fountains, they emerged through a labyrinth of rose-covered arbors into the bright light of two mighty torches, which were burning in cone-shaped sockets on the wall of the entrance to the mansion.

From the top of a stone stairway a tall, gray-bearded man, clad in a soft scarlet-striped tunic, his stalwart figure sharply outlined against the night, was watching Marcus as he approached slowly behind the servant. As Marcus paused at the foot of the stairs and looked up, his face was lighted by the giant torches.

"Marcus!" the man at the top of the stairway called in a voice filled with delight. And quickly he descended the broad steps to clasp the happy Marcus in his arms and said, "My house is honored indeed by your visit!" Slowly, arm in arm, the two soldiers ascended the stairs, passed through a wide vestibule and entered the atrium. Stepping to the wall, Cornelius pulled a bell cord to summon a servant, who appeared almost instantly.

He was an old, gray-haired man of medium build, and his movements, as he entered the room, were those of a man who had been buffeted by the storms of life. From under a high forehead shone a pair of clear and penetrating eyes, which Marcus recognized with a warm and friendly smile.

Cornelius looked at the old servant with an expression that betokened confidence and unquestioning trust in him as he laid a hand gently on his shoulders and said, "My dear Rufus, you probably remember young Marcus of the horse guard, with whom we shared many a danger in the days when we all were young and were enjoying the fullness of life. He has honored us with a visit, and I entrust him to your care."

Rufus bowed low before Marcus and said, "I am indeed honored to be remembered by the friend of my gracious master, and I shall delight in being of service to him."

The servant left at once to prepare a bath and to lay out a fresh tunic for the guest. Marcus, eager with the purpose of his mission, turned to the smiling Cornelius as if to speak, but was prevented by the latter from mentioning what was uppermost in his mind. "I know you have something on your mind, O Marcus," he said. "I can read it in your face. But that can wait, for Rufus is waiting for you. After you have had your bath, we shall sit down together once more as we have done many times in the past. Then we can talk to our heart's content."

Marcus nodded with a pleasant smile and said, "Forgive me, my friend, and I thank you for your kindness, but before I accept your hospitality, I must ask a favor of you, which, if granted, will lift a great burden from my heart."

Almost before Marcus concluded, Cornelius replied, "It is granted before I even know the reason for it. So speak that I may be of service to you."

Marcus quickly told his friend of his meeting with Jesup at Romar's inn and spoke of the despicable Obed, the horse trader. "All I ask of you," he continued, "is that you give me an opportunity to come face to face with this knave. I have instructed Jesup as to what he is to do, and I can trust him to see that Obed comes here."

After Marcus had told him the tragic story of David, Cornelius closed his eyes for a moment, then asked, "And this David; is he still alive?"

"That I do not know, my friend," Marcus answered. "But that is the chief reason for my wanting to lay hands on the Herodian. And if I do, I will force him to tell me what has become of David, or he will wish he had never seen the light of day!"

Cornelius, reading the vengeful look in the gray eyes correctly, shook his head, and said, "Marcus, I shall not break my promise to you. But let there be no bloodshed within the sanctuary of my house." And noting a look of disappointment in his friend's eyes, he added, "Please do not misunderstand me. There is no pity in my heart for the wretch; he deserves punishment. I only wish to say that this house of mine is a house of peace and not one of strife."

"I shall remember and respect your wish," Marcus nodded and left the atrium for the bath which Rufus had prepared.

A short time later he returned to the waiting Cornelius, who listened patiently to the plan which Marcus had conceived to trap the horse trader.

The two were about to leave for the dining room when the sound of the large gong was heard, telling them that Obed had arrived at the gate. Marcus hurriedly crossed the length of the atrium and hid in the heavy folds of the beautiful portieres that graced the entrance to the library. Cornelius remained and seated himself on a small marble bench a few steps away from the hidden Marcus.

Rufus entered shortly afterwards, announcing the horse trader. Before the servant left, Cornelius whispered a few words to him, then looked expectantly toward the door.

XIII

The Horse Trader

MARCUS, peering through the slightly parted portieres, was overcome with surprise when he saw Obed. "Why, this man," he said, "cannot be the sleek courtier who once served Herod!" And a feeling of pity for the fellow seemed almost to overcome him. His body seemed to consist of nothing but fat, that lay in heavy folds under the enormous neck, and as he came nearer, Marcus noticed how the corpulent stomach shook from the excess of accumulated fat. Costly rings glittered on his fingers as he stretched forth a greeting hand to Cornelius, who as yet made no effort to rise.

The centurion was well aware of the gleam of poorly concealed hatred that flickered for a second in the small black eyes of the trader, but he ignored it. "Noble Cornelius," the horse trader began, "pray forgive me for disturbing the peace of your house at such an unseemly hour, but if you will be kind enough to hear me for a moment, I will tell you the reason for my being here."

A slight nod from the old soldier bade him go on. "My servant Jesup," the horse trader continued, "returning from an errand in the town, told me of a horse he had seen that would be worthy of a king's ownership. Following its rider, he discovered that it belonged to you. He described the animal to me in such vivid and enthusiastic terms that I could not overcome the desire to see it immediately for myself. But I see my speech tires you," Obed smiled as he observed the look of impatience in the Roman's face, "never-

theless I rely on your noble and generous heart to hear me
out. The rich and poor in this city are all your friends, for
you make no distinction between them, and the Lord Almighty was indeed gracious when you were appointed to be
the guardian of law and order in Caesarea."

Cornelius, not misled by the unctuous flattery of the trader,
raised his brows in anger as he said, "Leave the name of God
Eternal out of your speech. Use it not for the praise of men."

Taken suddenly aback by the unexpected reprimand, Obed
looked strangely at Cornelius, a crafty gleam in his small,
malicious eyes, and said, "I am sorry if my words have
offended you, but I did not know of your strong feeling
toward your favorite God."

Cornelius, perceiving the tinge of irony in Obed's apology,
rose from his seat and answered cuttingly, "Your eyes reveal
to me the real truth about yourself. Why do you utter a lie,
when your wicked heart is telling you that I have spoken of
the only true and living God, a God apparently a stranger to
you. State your business and be done with it, for I find little
pleasure in continuing speech with you."

The horse trader knew that he had bungled and hated
himself for his own stupidity. To his question whether or not
the horse was for sale, Cornelius replied, "That is not for me
to decide. I do not own the animal, but I am willing to
oblige you, and I will call his owner."

Rufus appeared at his master's call and was instructed to
bring Marcus to the atrium. The servant went immediately
to the entrance to the lofty library, where Marcus had concealed himself in the folds of the portieres. But he found no
trace of him there. Seeing that the door which led out to the
garden was ajar, he stepped out and looked around.

Marcus, after Obed had entered, watched from his hiding
place and followed every word and movement of the trader;

and he also closely studied his old friend Cornelius. The latter was certainly a changed man. He now seemed to take everything so seriously. Nothing in the man reminded him of the carefree Cornelius he had known and campaigned with in years gone by.

Remembering his cue, when he saw old Rufus enter, he left his hiding place and went out into the garden. Why he went there, he did not really know, unless it was that he felt the need of getting one more breath of fresh air before he faced the Idumean.

A mellow moon had now risen, its silvery light revealing to him the beauty and perfect harmony of the well-kept garden. A hundred feet to his right stood a small round pavilion, its copper cupola reflected darkly in the pool of the fountain, where a flock of pigeons in the shadow of the pavilion bathed and cooled themselves during the hours of the noonday heat. Six marble steps led up to the structure, and a circle of benchlike seats made of dark-stained cedar ran along the balustrade.

Hearing the approach of Rufus, Marcus stood still for a moment, his eyes wandering aimlessly toward the pavilion, when he was startled at the sight of an old man standing motionless at the entrance. The man's right hand was closed tightly around a staff for support. The whole figure, with its snow-white hair playing softly in the night wind, and its flowing garment of white linen draped loosely around the frail body, presented to the astonished soldier a picture of a being that did not belong to earth. There seemed to be no life in the old man as he stood with closed eyes, his head bent slightly as if straining to identify a vaguely familiar voice.

While Marcus stood puzzled at the strange sight, Rufus approached and announced, "My master wishes to see you in the atrium."

Thanking him, Marcus pointed to the old man and inquired, "Rufus, who is this man?"

"I do not know his name, sir," Rufus answered. "No one does. My master, returning from a journey a few years ago, brought him here. He is only known to us as 'the servant of the King'."

The man standing on the marble steps of the pavilion began to move. Aided by his staff, he slowly descended and came toward them and, sensing the presence of Marcus, said, almost in a whisper, "The King is tarrying a little while on His way, but He will soon come."

A moonbeam, lighting the features of the aged man, revealed to the soldier a face marked by terrible suffering. Marcus, studying the eyes, noticed the wavering stare that is characteristic of the sightless. Slowly shaking his head in pity and bewilderment, Marcus turned away, resolved to ask Cornelius about the old man and to learn, if possible, more of his history.

XIV

"Where Is David?"

As Marcus entered, Cornelius rose from his seat and said, "Forgive me, my friend, for having sent for you, but you have Adallo to thank for the intrusion. It seems that he has found favor in the eyes of this gentleman," pointing to the grinning Obed. "He would like to purchase the horse from you."

With a cold, penetrating stare Marcus looked at the horse trader, and, as if annoyed at the mere thought of parting with his horse, he asked with a scowl, "And who, my good man, told you that I was willing to sell Adallo?"

For a moment Obed was silenced by the rebuff, but he quickly recovered and rejoined with mock cordiality, "Noble Roman, no one told me that he was for sale. But I think you would show poor judgment if you denied me the horse. You are a soldier, you know, and you might meet death at any moment. So why not sell me the horse now? I am ready to make a generous offer."

Marcus was tempted to laugh in the fellow's face, but he restrained himself and answered, "I see that you place great trust and faith in the word of your servant, to be in love with a horse your eyes have never seen."

"But you are wrong, my friend," the horse trader grinned. "I have already seen this Adallo. My servant pointed him out to me as we entered the estate by way of the stables."

Marcus stepped closer and looked sharply at the fellow, then answered with a cutting sneer, "I see that you have changed but little in your manner of doing business since we last met. You make certain to be on the profitable side of a transaction."

Vainly dissembling to conceal the growing suspicion that Marcus really knew something of his dastardly and treacherous past, Obed replied, "You are jesting, O Roman; we have never met before."

Despite the fixed smile of the horse trader, Marcus knew that the fellow's thoughts were disturbed and decided to give him no time to rally them. "Oh yes, we have met before," Marcus hastened to say. "My friend here," glancing at Cornelius, "did not tell you who I am."

Marcus paused for a moment, measuring the fellow, who became alarmed at the unwavering stare. "Who are you?" the trader finally asked, with a trace of fear in his voice as he cautiously retreated a few steps from Marcus.

"I am known as Marcus of the Procurator's Horse Guards at the Fortress Antonia in Jerusalem," Marcus answered, "and just to assist your memory, I will mention a few more names, the names of three men you have never been able to forget—three sheepherders named Asa, David, and Nathan!"

Fear and consternation shone in the deep-set eyes of the man as he struggled to master his feelings, and with much effort he replied, "You speak like a madman. How should I remember these men? I do not know them."

"Oh, but you do know them!" Marcus replied with a grin at the quaking horse trader, "for I happen to know your real name. You are Caleb, the former captain of the Household Guard of the late King Herod! Deny it if you will. But the fear in your guilty eyes gives me proof that I have spoken the truth."

Silence followed the soldier's words. The horse trader knew that he was trapped, and he looked around in desperation. But there was no help in sight. As he tried to moisten his dry lips, he vainly searched his tortured mind for a convincing reply. "How did this cursed Roman with the merciless eyes ever find out who I was?" he asked himself. He did not once suspect Jesup, his Syrian servant.

The incisive voice of Marcus broke into his chaotic thoughts, "I see you are confused and that you wonder how I happened to discover your identity. Your own covetousness and greed brought that about. For if your servant Jesup had not entered the Inn of the Gladiator with the desire of earning a few meager denarii from your hands, I probably would never have found you. But he did enter, and I, rescuing him from the punishing hand of Romar, recognized in him my old friend Jesup.

"I see you are surprised," Marcus went on, with a cold, satisfied look. "Yes, we have been friends, Jesup and I, ever since the days when you were still the favorite of Herod. And I presume," he added with sarcasm, "that you are acquainted with my friend Romar."

Helpless rage choked the horse trader as he was obliged to listen to the soldier. His narrow, selfish soul could not comprehend that it was not loyalty that bound the Syrian to him all these years, but that only the instinct of self-preservation had kept the servant from telling what he knew. For had Caleb been apprehended by the emissaries of Salome, Jesup, the trusted servant of the king's favorite, could hardly have escaped a similar fate.

At the mention of Romar's name the blood rushed hot to the face of the trader, who could not restrain a reply in his own defense. "The humiliation I suffered at Romar's hands I deserved not. That hot-tempered man attacked me before I could explain that my intentions toward his daughter were entirely honorable."

The cold, sarcastic smile of Marcus stopped him. "If

Romar knew you as I have known you, he was indeed justified in his manner of dealing with you. Unfortunately, poor Jesup, an unwilling tool of yours, was compelled to suffer the consequences. But enough of this. What I want to know from you is, what happened to my friend David? What have you done with him?"

Obed did not answer at once, for a terrible fear had overtaken him. The true reason he had been asked to visit Cornelius was now slowly dawning in his mind. Cringing before the fiercely angry eyes of Marcus, he fell to his knees, and with imploring hands he sought to justify himself before the two Romans as he pleaded, "I am an old man, O Roman. Let mercy rule your heart, for I am not guilty of the crimes of which you accuse me. It was by the order of Herod that your friends were taken into custody. It was no affair of mine."

"Your lies will benefit you but little," Marcus cut in relentlessly. "I care not by whose order David was arrested. All I want to know is, where is my friend?"

Cornelius was moved to sympathy for the poor fellow, but he declined to interfere.

Marcus continued, "Before you answer, let me add this to what I have already said. You are ignorant of the promise I gave to Elizabeth, the dying wife of David, that I would avenge all the suffering she was compelled to endure at your hands, if ever I found you. You and your satanic master were the cause of untold crimes which cry to heaven for vengeance. Herod is dead; but you are alive and here before me. Do not expect mercy from me. My vow to Elizabeth will see to that!"

The horse trader was a picture of desperation as he cowered at the feet of his tormentor, saying humbly, "I know, O Roman, that I am in your power, and I must bow to your will. I will give you a truthful answer. I know not what happened to David after I was forced to flee from Jerusalem. I cannot even give you the assurance that he is still alive." The dark and angry scowl of Marcus drove him on. "But there is a chance," he added, "that he is alive. For after my master's death, many prisoners were set at liberty. So why not David?"

"Yes, why not David?" Marcus said mechanically, forgetting the trader for a moment. "We do not know," he said to himself. "But if he was set free, how was he able to sustain himself, robbed of his sight as he was? No," turning to the trader, "you must give me a better answer, if you place any value on your life."

The Blind Man of the Pavilion

CORNELIUS had thus far kept silence, feeling that the affair between the two Romans did not concern him. But when he heard his friend's firm demand to the cringing trader he said, "Marcus, I ask you not to allow anger to cloud your sound judgment. I have reason to believe that this man has spoken the truth." Noticing the puzzled look in the eyes of Marcus, he went on to explain, "Withholding the truth would help this fellow but little in his present position. Have patience for a few moments, and I may be able to prove the sound sense of my words."

Before Marcus could answer, Cornelius pulled the bell cord, summoning Rufus, who, after Cornelius had whispered a few words to him, left hurriedly and returned a few moments later with the old man of the pavilion.

Cornelius glanced at the trader and, then turning to Marcus, said, "Here is the proof that my statement concerning the answer of this man was correct."

Marcus' eyes gleamed with excitement, and Cornelius smiled as he took the blind man by the hand, leading him over to Obed's side. Still holding the slender hand of the blind man, Cornelius said to him, "Tell these men, O servant of the King, for whom you are waiting."

The eyes of the two men were fixed on the impressive face of the old man as the answer came from his trembling lips, "I am waiting for the King who will redeem my people of Israel."

Cornelius noted with much interest the faces of the two men. The trader seemed unable to move; he stood as one paralyzed. His lower jaw sagged as his small black eyes were riveted on the marred face before him. And Marcus, looking at him, thought his behavior strange, for his deathly white face showed that he had sustained a terrible shock.

"It is he!" the trader cried hoarsely. "He is not dead; he lives!"

When fear and panic seized the trader, Cornelius stopped him as he attempted to rush from the room. Then, addressing Marcus, he pointed to the blind man and said, "For a number of years I have tried many times to learn the identity of this man, but have always failed. He still remained a man unknown to anyone. But I was wrong in giving up hope of finding out who he was, for He who rules the destinies of men willed that sometime I should know. And I have finally found the man who will be able to tell me his name."

Cornelius stopped and glanced anew at the trader and said, "The look in your fear-filled eyes tells me that you are that man. Now tell Marcus who this poor creature is."

Marcus needed no answer. He knew now that it was David who stood with unseeing eyes before him. His mind was filled with confused thoughts as he stepped close to the blind man to assure himself that he was not mistaken. But not a single feature in the blind man's face reminded him of the David he had known long years ago. Pity tugged at his heartstrings, and he shuddered as he gazed into the marred face, once filled with the glow of health and joy of youth.

Cornelius interrupted the sad thoughts of Marcus and said, "Let me explain, my friend, how I happened to know that this man was the David of whom you had spoken. Your story caused me to think of the nameless blind man I brought from Jerusalem many years ago. I found him lying in the gutter close by the sheep gate, a picture of poverty and despair. Pity for the man would not let me pass him by or deny him a helping hand. My trusted Nubians brought him here and cared for him. I realized at once that he was blind, and after a few weeks had passed, I learned also that he was a man without a memory. His mind was gone, probably lost under the strain and agony of torture. He seemed to be afflicted with an obsession, and the only words he ever spoke were these: 'I am the servant of the King who will redeem my people.'

"Why I have kept him throughout all these years I cannot tell. Perhaps it was that I saw him so utterly helpless. But now I know and realize that it was the hand of God that directed me to bring this David into my house."

As Cornelius spoke, Marcus frequently looked at Caleb, who stood waiting, with uncertainty and fear written in his face. The sight of the wretch, clothed in fine apparel, his fleshy fingers laden with costly rings, indicating his great wealth, drove the blood again to his head, as he thought of the sufferings and agonies of David and his loved ones. Yet Marcus was perplexed; he did not know how to proceed with Obed.

"What shall I do then with this fellow?" he said at last, looking at his friend. "Shall he go free, unpunished for all his dastardly work? No, he shall not! I will keep my promise to Elizabeth!"

Cornelius, with a soothing smile, interrupted, "Friend Marcus, let me ask you, would killing the knave bring back the sight to David's eyes? No. So why should you stain your hand with the blood of this man? Let the future determine his punishment, and leave him to the pangs of a guilty conscience."

Marcus looked for a long time at his friend without speaking. He could not quite understand the tender heart of Cornelius. Why was he inclined to show leniency where punishment was so clearly deserved? Seeing that further argument was ill-advised and guided by the desire to please his friend, he nodded slightly and said, "Perhaps you are right, Cornelius, it would profit me little to spill the fellow's blood, but there must be some way by which he can be made to suffer, and I think I have found it."

Turning to the loose-jowled Obed, Marcus continued, "My dear captain, listen carefully to what I have to tell you. It is only because of the love and respect I bear the noble Cornelius that I have decided to spare your life. But nourish no false hope that I have finished with you. Even though I have found David, there are still the memories of his sufferings at your hand. According to Jesup you are a man of wealth and enjoy the pleasures of life, while your servant must be satisfied with the crumbs that fall on occasion from your table of plenty. Of your servants I know only Jesup, but if I may judge their well-being by his appearance and condition, I fear you deserve little praise.

"Jesup was at all times a true friend to me, and my heart was deeply moved when I beheld him in misery at Romar's place. Upon my persistent urging, he reluctantly told me of the years of his fruitless desire to be a free man again and to live once more a normal life, free from fear and hunger. And," Marcus continued with a significant flicker in his eyes, "I promised him his freedom and the means by which he might end his remaining days in peace and contentment. And you, my fat friend, are now required to give him both. This will be but a small price for my leniency toward you." Marcus stopped for a moment to await the effect of his words and then continued, "You now have the choice to refuse my request and die, or to grant full freedom to Jesup and to go at once and get the sum of five thousand *sesterces,* which I will hand over to him as a token of your appreciation of his services to you. Which shall it be?"

The wretched man glanced for a moment from one to the other, drops of perspiration pearling on his forehead. But the icy stare from Marcus forced an answer from his quivering lips. "I am but a poor man, O Roman, and to fulfill your wish would make me a pauper indeed. But what other choice is there left to me?"

"Good," the soldier smiled, "I see that you understand the points of a good bargain. See that you keep your word, for if you plan to break it, you will have good cause to regret it. For there lives a man in Judea who would be willing to sell his soul for the chance of getting hold of you. Do not ask me his name, for knowing it would deprive you forever of your peace of mind."

Cornelius in the meantime had ordered Rufus to bring two guardsmen. He returned with two powerfully built Nubians, who looked to their master for instructions. Any plan for escape or flight that might have lingered in the mind of the Idumean was at once dispelled at the sight of these powerful men. Marcus told them what to do. A few minutes later the trader left with a Nubian on either side of him. Rufus, with a nod from Cornelius, led David away, and the two friends went to the dining room to enjoy the excellent meal which was served by willing and capable servants. They were joined a few minutes later by Jesup, who had been invited by Cornelius in honor of his release from poverty and slavery.

As they sat at their meal, Marcus could not help speaking of the newly found David and of the Divine Providence who had brightened his years of suffering through the kind and benevolent hand of Cornelius. "It seems to me," he said, looking at his friend across the table, "as if a Power, some Power unknown to me, stretched forth a protecting hand toward him when you beheld his misery years ago at the sheep gate."

"Your thoughts are justified indeed, my friend," Cornelius answered slowly. "There is such a Power, but you do not as yet know of its existence."

Marcus, in a way, knew to what his friend referred and thus voiced his thoughts, "You are a changed man, O Cornelius, and I wonder what has brought this about. You speak of a God invisible, a God whom no one has ever seen. How can one bring sacrifices to a God one is not able to see? All the gods I know and worship, my eyes can see. I know their dwelling places, and because I see them, I am able and willing to believe in them. But this God of whom you speak and whom no one has ever seen, I cannot trust. Show Him to me, and I promise you to serve and worship Him, if only for the sake of David."

An expression of pity as well as of disappointment clouded the features of Cornelius as he listened, and Marcus, perceiving this, continued humbly, "Forgive me, my friend, for my thoughtless and hasty words. Perhaps I do not understand it all as I should. It is all so new and strange to me and to my way of thinking. But tell me, why did this God of yours permit such dreadful suffering as David was forced to endure, if He is, as you say, all-powerful and wise? Why did He not stay the cruel hand of Herod?"

"Your questionings and doubts," Cornelius answered, "are the result of your ignorance of the ways of this God Eternal in His dealings with man. And I fear that you would still be in doubt after I have tried to explain them to you. But this I feel, and I earnestly pray, that the time is not far off when you will receive an answer to all your doubts and unbelief. And as to your remark that I am a changed man in many ways, I once more assure you that this too will be revealed to you in due time."

Jesup's questioning stare diverted their thoughts to other matters when he asked, "What are you planning to do with David, now that you have found him again? Do you intend to take him with you to Bethlehem? Is there still someone who would rejoice at his return?"

Marcus was not yet willing to reveal Dara's identity, but replied, "Yes, there is still someone, a near kinsman of David, who will gladly care for him and rejoice in so doing." His thoughts veered for a fleeting moment to Jason and pictured the latter's joy at seeing David once more. But a blind David! With a sorrowful sigh at the thought of it, he said to himself, "Oh, for the power that could bring back the light of day to those dead, sightless eyes!"

Without realizing it, he had voiced his thoughts aloud, but Cornelius, who was content to hope for something less than a miracle, said quietly, "Do not let your hopes rise too high. Be satisfied and thankful that David is alive. Take him back to the place of his birth, where he might recover his mind, if not his sight. Command me in anything that you may be in need of, and I shall be happy to be of service to you."

Marcus accepted the generous offer and said, "You are indeed a friend to all those who are in need. As soon as I have finished my official business, I will leave with David and Jesup. Until then, I will ask you to give my good friend Jesup shelter under your protecting roof, for I have but little faith in the word of a scoundrel like Caleb."

To this Cornelius replied, "Gladly will I grant your request. Jesup shall find protection and comfort in my house until you depart for Jerusalem."

With trembling lips the Syrian expressed his relief and gratitude.

XVI

Love, Sweet and Miserable

IT is late in the morning. In the little house at Bethany lies
Dara, still bedridden. But his wound is practically healed,
and he is well on the road to recovery. While he speaks,
Leonia, seated at the bedside, is patiently listening to
what he has to say. His hands, now lacking the healthy tan
of outdoor life, are playing restlessly with each other above
the bed covering as he says to her, "Tell me, sweet mother,
why does not Julian permit me to get up, so that I can leave
this detested bed? What reason can he have for keeping me
here like this? For I am almost well; my wounds are healed,
and I feel no pain." Then, incensed at the prolonged siege
of invalidism, he continues, "By Jupiter, I do not wish to lie
here any longer; I feel the need of exercise. But he keeps telling me that my legs are not yet strong enough to carry me."

Leonia listened to his every word with a patience which
only a mother's love can sustain. He did not know that every
one of his words added to the agony and pain that tore at
her heartstrings. She could easily have explained why Julian
had refused to allow him to get up. She had known for some
time that Julian feared the moment when Dara would
demand his release from the intolerable bed.

A sunbeam shining through the little window above the
bed played in the silver-tinted hair of the woman. Dara,
looking at her with adoring eyes, took one of her hands
lying idle in her lap, and struggling vainly to conceal his
worry, continued, "Mother dear, what I am about to tell
you may explain to you my reason for wanting to get up.

Despite the fact that my wounds are healed, I cannot throw off the dreadful thought that this bed will hold me down forever. It is these legs of mine that cause me to fear the worst. They are so heavy; and they seem to be without feeling. But, I keep asking myself, how could this wound in my back affect the use of my legs? I tell you, I cannot understand it. The fact remains, I cannot move them without the help of my hands. They seem to be paralyzed." And something like despair rang in his words as he ended, "O mother, what am I to do? What do you say?"

Leonia with difficulty restrained her tears as she beheld the anguish in Dara's face. Trying to hide the fact that she fully shared his apprehension, she said as soothingly as she could, "O Dara, your mind is distraught, and you are imagining dire things. Perhaps I should serve you with lighter food. You must have patience and wait for your legs to become stronger. I know it is difficult for you to lie still so long, for you are accustomed to a life of action. But you as a soldier should know how to obey without complaint."

To conclude the conversation that brought only pain and distress, Leonia rose from her seat and took a scarf from a wooden peg on the wall. Throwing it around her shoulders as she stood at the door, she turned to Dara and said, "I must leave you for a while, my son, to see what is detaining Rebecca. I hope she is not ill. Poor girl, I fear our coming here has burdened her with extra care and responsibility."

Returning a few moments later, she told Dara that she had not found the girl in the house. "She probably went into the town and will return soon," Leonia said as she looked at the disappointed youth, who fell back into the cushions without speaking.

A pang of deep distress shot through Leonia's breast as she contemplated the future. She knew that the two young people loved each other, but that both of them refrained from admitting it.

During the three weeks since Marcus had left for Caesarea, Rebecca cared for Dara during the day, when Leonia would rest and sleep, thus being refreshed and ready for her hours of duty at night. It was during the trying hours of these first days with Dara that the girl lost her heart to the young soldier. But happy though she was for the moment, her situation made her miserable. For how would it end? She, a humble Hebrew girl, and he, a proud Roman, part of the mighty Empire that held her beloved land under the iron heel of a conqueror! Yet, she admitted to herself, there were exceptions; for there were Marcus and Silvanus. But this thought helped her but little in solving the problem that filled her mind and soul. The gulf between them seemed too great to be bridged even by a love as strong as theirs.

A week or so later, Dara had improved to such an extent that it was no longer necessary for anyone to be with him at night. In a way, Rebecca was thankful for this. She wanted to escape to fight her feeling for the young man, the feeling that had robbed her of sleep and of peace of mind. Countless times she had tried to tear this love from her heart, but had always failed. Whenever she entered the sickroom and beheld the soft brown eyes of the smiling Dara gazing at her with lingering glances of warmest affection, she became oblivious for the time of her perplexing situation and yielded again to the spell of happiness which his smile invariably cast over her.

Her heart filled with emotion, the young girl left the house one morning to seek the help and advice of her friends, Mary and Martha, who, together with their brother Lazarus, lived a short distance down the road. Hastening along the narrow path that led to Martha's house, she shook her scarf-covered head in perplexity and said to herself, "Why do Leonia and Dara seem so good? And why do I love his mother as if she were my own?" Recalling her motherless childhood, she found it a comfort to think of Leonia as taking the long vacant place of her own mother.

Suddenly, as weeping voices came to her ears, she stopped to listen. With a startled cry she hurried the rest of the way, anxious to learn the cause of the mournful voices that grew louder as she came nearer to Martha's house.

XVII

Lazarus Is Dead

THAT Lazarus and his sisters were persons of comfortable means could be readily seen by their moderately pretentious estate. The house stood at some distance from the main thoroughfare of the town. A well-kept tract of garden fronted the house, its hedges trimmed in perfect patterns. Roses of Sharon bloomed along the white sandstone walls of the house. Lilies of the valley, planted along the gravel paths of the garden, vied in beauty with the crimson anemones growing in colored pots of clay arranged on the broad window sills.

To the left of the house was a terraced gallery, its roof covered with vines of wild ivy. Stone benches ran along the pillar supports of the roof. Trays of delicious fruit on the linen-covered cedar table invited the visitor to refresh himself.

Rebecca looked through the partly opened door as she stopped at the entrance to the house, and a premonition gripped her heart. With a hesitant step she entered and found the spacious room crowded with friends and neighbors of the two sisters. Some of them knelt before a bier standing in a corner, upon which lay the body of Lazarus, his hands folded over a silent breast. Deep sorrow filled the girl's heart as she looked at the dead man. Near by stood Martha, whose tear-stained face showed the agony in her heart. As Rebecca went to comfort her, she heard the poor woman weeping and repeating the words, "If only the Master had come, my brother would not have died!"

For a moment a picture came to Rebecca's mind, a picture

of the Master as she had seen Him at the Feast of Taber-
nacles when He tarried a few days at the home of Martha.
At her friend's invitation she had come to hear Him speak.
Never had anyone affected her so profoundly, and His voice
had a quality that she would always remember.

Trying to console the woman in her woe, Rebecca said,
"Perhaps the Master did not know of your brother's sickness,
otherwise He surely would have come."

Martha shook her head and said, "He knew of it. My faith
tells me it could not have been otherwise, for nothing is ever
hidden from Him. And He loved my brother."

A few moments later a younger woman, beautiful and soulful, stepped away from the bier and joined Rebecca and
Martha, taking the latter by the hand. It was Mary, Martha's
younger sister. As Rebecca looked at her, she thought it
strange that Mary's face showed no sign of tears or grief.
Curious to know the reason for such unusual composure,
Rebecca was moved to inquire, "Why do you show so little
grief, my dear, at the loss of your brother? Do you not feel
your great loss? I see your face free from tears and your
eyes bright with hope."

It was Martha who answered, "Mary clings to the hope
that our brother will be restored to us by the grace of the
Master. But this cannot be, for Lazarus is dead."

Mary then studied the sad face of the girl for a moment
and replied with a hopeful smile, "My grief, O Rebecca,
lies buried in the depth of my heart, and I will not let it
rise, for I am cheered and comforted by the glorious hope
that my brother will rise again. I know the Master loved him,
and I sincerely believe that He can and will restore Lazarus
to us."

"But what can He do, this Master?" the girl asked excitedly. "Your brother is dead. The Master surely cannot

bring him back to life! That would be impossible!"

"Nothing is impossible with Him, my dear," Mary replied, strong in her faith. "Did He not restore the dead son of the widow at Nain when He beheld the agonizing sorrow of the bereaved mother? So why should I doubt and lose faith in Him who could still the raging tempest of the sea by His words 'Be still'? He surely will have pity for the sorrow of my sister and for the pain in my tearless eyes."

A tempest of emotion in Rebecca's heart was stilled as she looked into the face of her friend, whose quiet hope enkindled in her own heart a full assurance of the Master's help.

After assisting with the preparation for the burial in the family sepulcher, and before the shadows of eventide darkened the town, Rebecca returned to her home, unaware that her absence had needlessly distressed Leonia and Dara.

"Where have you been, my child?" Leonia said with a sigh of relief. "Dara and I were at a loss to explain your long absence from the house. I hope that nothing has happened to your father." Rebecca, reproaching herself for the worry she had thoughtlessly caused, then told them the reason for her absence and, after concluding the account, retired to her own room.

For a long time after the girl had left, there was not a sound to be heard in the room, except the occasional noise of the grazing horse which Marcus had left in place of Adallo. Leonia, seated on a low stool by the bed, looked up into the brooding face of her son and asked with much concern, "Why are you so quiet, my son? Is there something wrong?"

"No, mother, there is nothing wrong," Dara answered; "but I have a perplexing question on my mind which I am afraid to ask for fear you may misunderstand me."

Leonia smiled as if to encourage the boy and said, "No,

my son, why should I ever withhold an answer if you are in need of it? What is it you wish to know?"

"Mother," he began, looking shyly at her, "Would you have married my father if he had not been a Roman? Please try to understand. I ask not out of curiosity, but for a reason which, with due respect to your feelings, I should prefer not to divulge, at least for the present."

Leonia noticed that the question had caused him much embarrassment and asked with a smile, "Dara, do you still trust your mother?"

"That I do," Dara answered. "But why do you ask?"

"Because," his mother answered in a tone of mild reproof, "I think you are withholding something from me. I was ever happy in the thought that your heart belonged to me and to me alone. To whom did you confide when you were a little boy? Or to whom did you come when your little heart was troubled? Was it not your mother who comforted you then? Why should I not now have the privilege to comfort you?"

A flush of embarrassment showed in the boy's face as he replied rather timidly, "This matter is different. I cannot now explain it as fully as I should like to," Dara replied.

Leonia, noting the boy's diffidence, thought it wise not to press the matter further. And looking at him with a knowing smile, she said, "My son, I would have married your father had he been only a lowly shepherd. True love, my son, does not weigh such matters. For love is one of the most precious gifts of God to mortals. Ask your heart only, and be sure that this love of yours is strong enough to surmount every obstacle in its path, and happiness will surely be yours."

His adoring eyes told her more than his words that she had indeed made him happy by her answer.

XVIII

"Come . . . Walk"

THE following morning, just as Dara had finished the breakfast which Leonia had brought him, Julian, who had left only a few days before, arrived unexpectedly. For a moment Leonia's surprise and pleasure at his return brightened into a smile, but it passed quickly when she noticed the uneasiness and suppressed anxiety which the doctor, with an air of buoyant optimism, tried in vain to conceal. With the feeling that her most dismal fears were about to be realized, she turned with a pleading look to the doctor, who, just as she began to speak, interrupted her by saying, "Dara, my friend, I have come to see if you can walk. You can try, anyway, although I fear your legs are still a little weak. But we shall see."

Julian, noting an expression of anxiety in Leonia's eyes, said no more for the moment. Dara, unaware of their exchange of foreboding glances, laughed happily as he asked for his tunic. Dropping the garment over his shoulders, he pushed back the bedcovering and, with the help of the little doctor, lifted his legs over the edge of the bed. With a forced laugh that betrayed his mixed emotions of joy and fear, he said, as if for self-encouragement, "After all, perhaps mother was right. These legs of mine seem very weak and helpless. But I will succeed yet!" He spoke on, trying at the same time to gather strength to fight the dark fear that threatened to overwhelm him. With Julian's assistance he managed to stand upright. The doctor stepped quietly aside, intently studying the face of his patient, and then said with a tone of gentle authority, "Come, Dara . . . Walk!"

Leonia, almost hopeful, stepped to Dara's side and took hold of his arms to help him in his effort to stand up. At the words of Julian, "Come . . . Walk," she could feel the strain and effort in his arm muscles as he tried to obey. Drops of perspiration formed on his forehead, and grim determination tightly closed his lips. The doctor's words seemed to mock him. "Come . . . Walk!" Did he not know that this was impossible! His legs felt as if they were glued to the floor!

For a fleeting moment his thoughts turned to Rebecca. "For her sake I must walk!" he said to himself with renewed courage. But the muscles of his legs still refused to respond to the inner command, and he collapsed in a heap beside the bed. With the help of Leonia, Julian lifted him back into the bed.

Leonia perceived the boy's distress as she saw the discouraged look on his pale face. Julian, with a tone of most profound sorrow in his voice, turned to the boy and said, "Dara, my boy, what I am compelled to tell you now will be a shock to you as well as to your mother. But you must know the truth. You will probably never walk again! Your legs are paralyzed! There is no hope. Only through some miracle can the use of your legs be restored to you."

Before Dara could grasp the full import of the doctor's words, a voice from the opened door was heard: "And this miracle, O noble Dara, will surely happen."

Softly but firmly these words came from the lips of Rebecca as she noiselessly closed the door behind her. Her usual shyness seemed to have left her as she drew closer to the bed, looking with tenderness at the saddened face of the young Dara. "My friend," the girl smiled, "I heard the words of good Julian, and I know they have brought you sorrow. But I ask you not to despair. You are sick and helpless now, but I assure you this condition will last only a short time."

Leonia stared at the girl with an expression of incredulity. She could not comprehend the meaning of the girl's words. Rebecca knew this and, trying to allay the woman's doubt, said, "Good lady, I understand your doubt, and I chide you not for it. All I ask now is that you trust me. For I would not arouse in you any false hope concerning your son. I will tell you more of all this after my return from Bethany, where I must go again this morning. I may be late in returning, but if it is God's will, I shall return with good tidings."

"We shall be waiting for you, my dear," Leonia said as the girl left the room.

Julian had remained silent thus far, but when the door closed behind the girl, he remarked dryly to Leonia, "I hope, Leonia, that you do not place too much hope in the senseless promises of the girl. For I should like to know how she will be able to keep her promise. So far as I can see, only a miracle can help Dara; and I do not believe in miracles."

Leonia did not answer; with her eyes on the bed, she observed the relaxed features of her son, which assured her that he trusted and believed Rebecca's promise. Then, turning to Julian, she said, "Tomorrow, my friend, we may be able to dissipate your doubts."

This did not fully satisfy the little man, and, still firm in his opinion, he replied, "Very well, dear Leonia, I shall look forward to tomorrow, but in the meantime. . . ." Suddenly the doctor stopped. Turning his head, he stood listening. He had heard the shout of a horseman pulling his mount to a stop before the garden gate. Recognizing the familiar voice of his friend, he went at once to the door and exclaimed, "Silvanus is here!"

XIX

One Mystery Solved

As Silvanus walked through the door, he dropped his helmet and plaid upon the small wooden bench near the entrance. He stepped to the bedside of his young friend and, in a jovial tone of voice that deceived no one, said, "Why are you still in bed, Dara? It seems to me that you enjoy being nursed and pampered, else you would be up! Or is there some other reason for your remaining in bed!"

His twinkling eyes forced a wry smile from Dara, but he did not answer at once, for Leonia had tugged gently at the arm of Silvanus and asked, "Is there any news from Marcus?"

"I am sorry, my dear friend," Silvanus answered; "no news as yet. But considering the time he has been gone, we may expect him now any day." Then, turning to Dara, he again questioned him regarding his condition. Laughing nervously, the boy pointed with a shaky finger to Julian and said, "Let him tell you. But do not blame him for my condition, for he has done all he could for me."

With a tone of alarm in his voice, the old soldier faced the little doctor and asked, "What does the boy mean by saying that I should not blame you?"

Julian told Silvanus what he thought about Dara's condition and felt sorry when he noticed how his words affected the old soldier. With a questioning look Silvanus turned to Leonia, whose eyes were now filled with tears when she said, "Do not trust too much in his words, Silvanus. Dara will not remain like this forever. Sweet Rebecca promised me this, and I have fullest confidence in her words."

Jason, who had meanwhile quietly entered the room, remained standing near the door as the two were speaking. Hearing Leonia's confident assertion, he drew close to her and said, "I thank you, O lady, for your trust in my child. I do not know what grounds sustain her hope, but I am sure we shall not be disappointed."

Silvanus heard but little of all this, for his sorrow for Dara had almost overwhelmed him as he eyed the young man. No one but himself could feel that all of his hopes for Dara, all that he had long worked for, now lay shattered at his feet. His heart cried out that this could not be! Dara must walk! This noble young man should not remain a cripple!

The doctor, leaning with an elbow on the window sill, happened to be looking out, gazing idly at the hills whose rocky slopes bordered the dusty old caravan road to Jericho. "Look!" he exclaimed. "Behold who is coming!" The cry brought them all rushing to the small window to see Marcus astride the back of Adallo. The dark cloud of discouragement that had a moment before filled the room seemed at once to vanish as they rushed toward the door.

A few minutes later Marcus swung out of the saddle and embraced the sobbing Leonia. The soldier looked at her with uneasiness and, beholding her tear-stained face, inquired anxiously, "Is Dara all right?"

The expression of her face changed quickly at the words of her husband, and her smile dispelled any dark thoughts about the boy that had disturbed his mind. Then his attention was drawn suddenly away from Leonia by the excited cry of Julian. "What on earth have we here?" the little man exclaimed, his fingers pointing to a group of three horsemen, two of whom were Nubians bearing a burden.

"They are my friends," Marcus said with a smile, shaking

the hands of Silvanus and Jason. "And," he went on after a slight pause, "prepare yourselves for a great surprise!"

The three riders halted at the gate, and the foremost of them, a dark-skinned Syrian, dismounted slowly and remained standing at the head of his mount. Silvanus drew closer as he glanced at him, recognizing his old friend, and cried, "Jesup! Jesup!"

With a deep smile in his face, the Syrian responded to the warm greeting as he felt the strong handclasp of the soldier and said, "Yes, my friend, it is I, Jesup, who stands before you."

Julian's eyes bulged with curiosity as he looked at the two men. He seemed to sense something portentous in their arrival.

The two husky Nubians, at a nod from Marcus, loosened the enclosed litter that was suspended between their horses and deposited it at Jason's feet. Everyone became curious now as Marcus, not wholly unaware of his role in the dramatic moment, stepped to the side of the old herder and said, "Jason, my friend, lift the curtain of this litter and tell me who that man is." At these words of the soldier the herder pushed the curtains apart. From the interior of the litter came a dead, toneless voice which said, "I will not betray Thee, O my King!"

The herder stood in mute astonishment as he listened, his glance turning to Marcus and then again to the face of the speaker. A tremor ran through his body as he tenderly lifted the silvery head of the man from its cushions. The next moment the herder sank to his knees before the litter, pressing the gentle face of the man to his breast. "David, O David, you have finally come back home to me!" he sobbed in a voice half-choked and trembling with emotion.

Leonia and Silvanus stood silent, too deeply moved to

speak a word. The little doctor eased his pent-up surprise and elation with the remark: "If one desires to witness the performance of a miracle, let him visit the house of Jason!" At these words, Jason said softly. "Yes, my friend, it does seem like a miracle that my David is restored to me. By the grace of the Almighty this has been brought about."

David was now carried into the house; the others followed, anxious to hear from Marcus how he had been able to find the old man. Leonia, with the help of Jason, hastened to serve food and refreshments to the weary travelers. Every step of Jason, as he moved about, told of the happiness that now surged in his heart. Marcus and Silvanus could discern in the old herder the rebirth of a soul that once had tasted the bitterest hardships of life.

With a motherly tenderness Jason lifted David from the litter and seated him gently on a chair by the large cedar table, where he was soon enjoying a lunch of hot biscuits and warm goat's milk. Jason, until now unaware of the absence of his daughter, inquired of Leonia where she was. Leonia acknowledged the question but did not answer at once. She knew that the herder was ignorant of the death of his neighbor Lazarus and hesitated to tell him about it. She also knew from Rebecca of his great love for his friend. But when she noticed the look of alarm in his eyes, she thought it best for him to know and said, "My friend, Rebecca is well, but is stricken with grief. Your friend Lazarus died but yesterday, and Rebecca has gone to Bethany to comfort his sisters in their bereavement."

This shook the herder. After recovering from the first shock at the sad news, Jason bowed his head in resignation and said, "But I have found a friend today in return for the one whom the Lord has taken from me."

Marcus, after watching Dara's face for some time, drew

the doctor to one side and asked him why the boy was still confined to his bed. Julian wished himself back in Jerusalem as he looked at the soldier and complained under his breath, "Why should I always be the bearer of bad news!" Then, noticing the imploring look of Leonia and Dara, he told Marcus in a few words what he thought was wrong with the boy. Not a muscle in the soldier's stolid face told of the pain that pierced his heart and mind as he heard the dire words of the doctor.

His eyes now sought Jesup, who was in conversation with Silvanus. At a motion from Marcus, the Syrian followed him to the front of the house. Marcus sat on the stone bench like one who is very tired, yet knows there is still much to be done. Soon, however, he turned to the Syrian and offered him the company and protection of the two Nubians for the remainder of the journey to his homeland, where he could spend his remaining years in full enjoyment of the freedom that Marcus had secured for him. Then, reaching into a pocket, Marcus brought forth the bag of money which he had forced from the miserly hands of Caleb and handed it to him and said, "A small token from your former employer in appreciation of your faithful service to him!"

The Syrian stood speechless, and tears of thankfulness welled up in his eyes as he received the bag from the hand of his benefactor. Marcus, seeing the joy in the face of Jesup, felt much of the weight of his own sorrow lifted from his soul.

Soon afterwards the Syrian, with the good wishes of his friends, who gathered around him, left with the Nubians as his bodyguard. Julian had gladly agreed to accompany him as far as Jerusalem. Before the riders disappeared down the road, Marcus, Leonia, Silvanus, and the blind David returned into the house to join Dara, who had been left alone with his thoughts. Jason, however, lingered at the gate.

Though not a word was spoken, each knew that the others were quietly awaiting the return of Rebecca, who was expected at any moment.

XX

Rebecca's Story

Just after the others had entered the house, Jason saw Rebecca coming through the garden gate of Martha's home. He went part way down the hill to meet her. The girl clung to his arm as she told him of the sorrow of the two sisters.

"My child," her father said as he tried to soothe her, suppressing the ache that pulsed through his own breast, "great is their trouble, but great is the mercy of the Lord, and He surely will comfort and sustain them in their sorrow."

When they arrived at the house, they found the others gathered in Dara's room. Slowly the girl seated herself beside Leonia and, as if ashamed to show her grief so openly, turned to her father and said, "Father, may I speak to you all, for I have news of the utmost importance."

"Speak, my child," the herder said softly, "and may your words be a blessing to us all."

With a smile of thanks she turned from him to face Leonia, taking her by the hand, and said, "Dear lady, do you remember the starlit night of a few weeks ago and the wish your lips breathed into the silence of that night?"

"I do," the woman answered softly, "and the Almighty has granted my wish, for Dara did not die!"

Rebecca, pleased at Leonia's answer, looked for a moment at the faces before her, then began to tell them of her visit to the sisters. "I found Martha filled with grief," she began, "but Mary, the beautiful one, seemed to have overcome her sorrow, for she had even a cheerful smile for me as she greeted me at the door. I wondered at this lack of grief, which was so clearly manifested in the tear-filled eyes of her sister. Martha, seemingly trying to forget her sorrow, busied herself in the kitchen, baking and cooking, as though preparing for some important visitor. 'Whom do you expect, my dear?' I asked her. 'The Master,' she answered. 'Had He been here these last three days, this sorrow would not have visited our home.' I wondered who this Master really was.

"Mary in the meantime had gone to the patio, where I found her watering the flowers that were arrayed in pots on the broad window sills. I watched her for a while, then asked, 'Mary, who is the Master? Please tell me about Him.' She smiled at me, and, putting the watering jug down upon the ledge that ran along the wall, she asked me to sit down beside her. Then she answered softly, 'He is the promised Messiah of Israel,' and, noting an expression of wonder in my face, she explained at greater length so that I might be able to understand more clearly. 'He is the Man spoken of by the prophets, the Man who shall sit on the throne of David and redeem our people from bondage. I know that He will indeed be able to accomplish this, for does He not show His mighty power in the wonders and miracles performed by Him? No other man has been able to do such things.' Mary then told of the miracles He had performed in the course of His wanderings about the country."

"Does He then heal anyone who asks of Him to be healed?" Leonia interrupted at this moment. Does not one need to pay Him for His services?"

Slightly confused for a moment by the interruption, Rebecca glanced at Leonia and continued, "Mary told me that He healed all those who believed in His power and were born of the seed of our father Abraham."

"Then there is no chance for me, a Roman?" Dara asked

in a tone of disappointment.

At Dara's question the girl was almost overcome by the feeling of her own helplessness. Yet her love for Dara caused her to speak whatever words of promise and encouragement she was able to summon to her help. "I have spoken to Mary about your misfortune," she said.

"And what did she say?" Leonia asked, pressing the girl's hand with her own moist fingers. "Is there a chance for my boy?"

"Yes," the girl answered confidently, "for Mary has promised me that she will intercede for him with the Master. And to strengthen your hope," Rebecca continued with a smile, "I will tell you a story of a woman, not a Jewess, whose daughter the Master healed, because she never faltered in her faith in Him. She was a Canaanite from the city of Tyre. Her child was beset with evil spirits. The Master at first seemed to ignore her cries. His little company of disciples, annoyed at the woman's persistence, begged Him to send her away. Then He answered them and said, 'I am not sent but to the lost sheep of Israel. It is not right to take bread from the children and give it to dogs.'

"The woman was not discouraged and cried, 'That is true, O Lord, yet the dogs eat of the crumbs which fall from their master's table.' At this humble reply, the Master granted the woman her wish, saying, 'Thy faith is great, O woman; be it unto thee as thou wilt.' And her daughter was healed forthwith."

As Rebecca related this story, her listeners naturally weighed the possibility of Dara's being cured of his affliction. And the girl shared these thoughts when she drew closer to the bed and said, in a voice soft and encouraging, "Noble Dara, would it not be wonderful if we could see you walk again? And you will walk again if you believe from the depth of your heart that He is the Messiah, the Redeemer of Israel." Noting the doubtful expression of the two old soldiers, she continued, "It may be difficult for some to believe in the origin of the Master. His mother's name is Mary. Her husband, named Joseph, is a carpenter in the town of Nazareth in Galilee. This Jesus (that is His name), her first-born, was born in a cave near Bethlehem, for there was no room found for them at the khan when they arrived for the taxing over thirty years ago. It was only through the tender heart of the innkeeper, who recognized in Joseph a descendent of the kingly house of David, that room was found for them in one of the caves where the innkeeper kept his cattle. And there she gave birth to her first-born.

"To my question, 'How do you know that He is really the promised Messiah?' Mary answered, 'I know, for my eyes have seen Him, and my heart tells me that He is the Messiah. But to give you better proof that He is the Messiah, I will tell you what happened at the hour of His birth. Shepherds guarding their sheep at night were told by the angel of the Lord that their Savior was born; and that, as a sign unto them, they would find the Babe lying in a manger, wrapped in swaddling clothes'."

Dara, who had lain quiet, his eyes fixed on the lovely features of the girl, interrupted her again and asked, "Tell me, dear Rebecca, did those shepherds go, and did they find Him as they were told they would?"

The girl's face wore a puzzled look as she turned to him, for she could not answer his question. Dara noticed her embarrassment and sought to put her mind at ease and said, "I did not ask this, O Rebecca, to satisfy my curiosity. But the thought came to me that one could more readily believe in this man, whom you call Master, if it could be proved by actual witnesses that He is the Babe of the manger."

"O Dara," his mother cried, "why do you doubt? Why can you not believe when you are told of the miracles wrought by the Master?"

Young Dara still felt uncertain as the eyes of the two women were directed toward him, and before he could speak further, Jason stepped to the foot of the bed and raised his right hand as if to draw the attention of the young man and said, "Son, your question comes from a reasoning heart, and I condemn you not for it." After a slight pause the herder continued, "I can give you an answer to your question. There are still living two of those shepherds who were present on that eventful night of which my child just spoke. One of them stands before you! The other one is this blind man whom Marcus brought back from Caesarea!" Rebecca, absorbed in her own story, had failed to take notice of David. "There were three, but one is dead. He paid with his life for his loyalty to the newborn King, because he would not deliver Him into the hands of Herod, the tyrant. But this will all be told to you in due time."

This revelation, coming so unexpectedly from the old herder, caused a stir of wonder and astonishment in the hearts and minds of all the listeners. Marcus, Leonia, and Silvanus were perhaps less surprised than Dara and Rebecca, for they had already known something, if not the whole truth, of the wonderful story just told by Jason.

Rebecca looked at her father with eyes filled with wonder as he spoke. Not until her father had called attention to David, was she aware of the presence of the blind man whom she saw sleeping on a quickly improvised bed. Occupied as she was with other matters, she had made no inquiry about him, not even when she thought she had heard him mumble something about a King.

The girl knew that with her father's revelation another

side of his life and character, so far unknown to her, would be eventually unfolded to her, and her eyes sought an explanation of it all as she looked up inquiringly at him. Her father understood her silent plea and decided to tell her the story of his life. But not for a moment did he forget his promise to Leonia, to guard Dara's real identity, feeling that there would come a time when he would be free to make it known to her.

In a voice filled with bitter memories, he told her of his youth; of his life with Asa and David; of the eventful hour of the birth of the Master. He told her also of his fight at Asa's camp, where he tried to frustrate Herod's devilish plan of destruction; and of the death of the husky Thracian.

Dara's gaze was fixed on the old bearded face, and a feeling of admiration and deep respect for the old man filled his heart as he listened to Jason's words. This was not merely the kind and tender herder he had known. No, there stood before him a man who had suffered the woes of a martyr, one who had been robbed of nearly everything that was dear and precious to him.

When his daughter, choking with grief, begged her father to stop, Jason ended his story by saying, "Since I knew that I would be recognized eventually and hunted down as a murderer, I decided to leave Bethlehem. Your dear mother and I settled here at Bethany, and I assumed another name, the name of Jason."

The old man stopped, his large hands softly caressing the bowed head of his child, and, looking earnestly at Dara, he added, "All that I have said will be confirmed by your father and Silvanus, who were united in friendship with Asa, David, and myself, yea, long before your time." Then, after another short pause, he turned directly to Dara and said, "Are you willing to believe in the Master and His power, and with it regain your health? Or would you rather, by rejecting Him, forfeit His help and remain a cripple all the days of your life?"

Every eye turned to the young man, who looked with indecision from one to the other. Jason, further to encourage the young man, added, "By tomorrow, my son, when Jesus the Master arrives at the home of Martha, I will be there. I will be waiting for Him, and I will seek His mercy for David that He may give back the light of day to his unseeing eyes, and I myself will pay Him homage."

Still the boy was silent. Leonia and Marcus rose and came to the bedside. The warm grip of his hand gave her courage to speak. Looking pleadingly at her son, she said, "We too will be there, good Jason. Will we not, Dara? I care not if, beholding me, a Roman, He should turn in displeasure from me, as long as He makes my son whole again. But my heart is filled with the hope and belief that He, yea only He, will be able to take the sorrow from my heart and restore to Dara the use of his legs."

Their conversation ended, Jason left the house to visit the sisters of his dead friend Lazarus, and the faithful Rebecca hastened to the bedside of David, who had just awakened from a restful sleep, to add to his comfort and happiness.

XXI

Marcus Reasons with Silvanus

ARCUS and Silvanus had gone to the front of the house, where they were seated on the sandstone bench that stood near the door. Their thoughts were centered on Dara and his affliction, and on their old friend now resting in the house. After a long silence Marcus startled his brooding friend Silvanus by suddenly saying, "To think that I, whom Dara calls his father, should find the man who has the only true claim to that name! But there he is, the David who once walked by our side in all the glory of his youth, sitting there, his sightless eyes staring into eternal night, not knowing that his own son, whom he has not seen since he was a little child, is under the same roof with him!"

Slightly irritated at the interruption of his own thoughts, Silvanus sighed and said, "What on earth do you mean? Why speak of things that cannot be changed or mended?"

Marcus, annoyed at his friend's discouraging attitude, replied somewhat angrily, "But you are wrong, Silvanus, for some things can be changed."

"How?" Silvanus, smiling, rejoined in a challenging tone. "How can you change the infirmities of Dara? Do you expect a miracle to happen?"

"That I do, my friend," Marcus nodded with conviction. "And to bring this about, we must tell the boy who he is, since the mercy of Jesus is only for the Jews. And I fear the consequences. What will be the effect on him, whom we have brought up in the way of a Roman, when he learns that he is a Jew, when he learns that the woman he adores is not his real mother? I tell you the whole matter weighs heavily on my heart."

Silvanus, with a show of some annoyance, turned about, looking straight at Marcus, and said, "Nonsense, why do you worry that this will affect the boy? My advice to you is that you tell him nothing. How do you know," Silvanus continued, "that this so-called Master can bring about this miracle? You had better be careful and wait until we know more about this Man. My eyes must first see before I will believe in such things. I ask you, who has ever heard that the dead can rise from their graves and a blind man regain his sight?"

Marcus found no ready answer to his friend's question, and for a while he said nothing. Finally he looked sternly at his companion and replied, "Silvanus, listen to me. Would it really be such a terrible shock to the boy to learn that he is the son of a Jew? Tell me, what glories have we ever found from the life that we have led all these years? Perhaps the satisfaction that we were a part of this mighty Empire; perhaps the knowledge that we took part in the building of mighty Rome, the mistress of the world! But are we really contented? Your eyes tell me No. And I have thought this for some time. You have begun to hate the role of a soldier since you have seen Dara lying in the bed to which he is still confined. You were always a realistic man, Silvanus, and you would never believe anything you did not see for yourself. And it is this fact that troubles you now. Your heart begs you to believe, if not for your own sake, at least for the sake of the boy whom you love. But your pride prevents you from believing.

"You are a Roman first of all, and you have little confidence in anyone who is not a Roman. Therefore you are not willing to put your trust in the person and power of a Jewish healer whom your eyes have never seen. This is the cause of your unhappiness. I know, for I have had the same experience myself. But my love for Dara and his blind father caused me to change my attitude and to believe in this Jesus. And I will tell you how this came about. Do you remember the night we found Elizabeth dying by the roadside? And do you recall her prophetic words concerning her loved ones, that David would some day behold the face of his son again?

"Well," Marcus went on, "we all gave David up as dead. And now, many years later, David's own son, lying near death in the road, was found by his only surviving kinsman, whom we also thought dead. I ask you, is this not the working of a power which we are not able to comprehend; a power by which the words of the dying Elizabeth are about to be fulfilled? If Jason had not found him, you would never have known him as the kinsman of David. Furthermore, I, who had not been in Caesarea for years, was suddenly sent there with dispatches for the procurator. And with the desire to see justice done at Romar's Inn, I found Jesup, who led me eventually to Caleb and later to David.

"And now, my friend," Marcus concluded, with a note of confidence in his voice, "when I consider all these things, and when I listen to the story of Rebecca and her father about the Galilean, a new hope and belief fills my heart. You know as well as I do that there is no help or hope for the boy except through some miracle; and I believe in all sincerity that my boy will walk again, by the grace of this great Healer. That is the reason why we must tell Dara whose son he is."

Silvanus shook his head as if to imply that he was not yet convinced of the necessity for this and said, "If this Master is really so all-powerful, He surely will know the parentage of the boy, and if He does, I give you my solemn word that I then will believe in Him and His power. But until then, I cannot believe."

Having accomplished little by the rather heated discussion, both men thought it wiser to drop the matter for the time being and to remain silent. As they thus sat side by side, saying nothing, both felt greatly relieved when they saw Jason coming slowly up the hill toward the house. Rising from their seats, they remained standing until he stopped before them. Jason's face was wreathed in a smile that reflected his innermost feelings as he said, "The Master will be here tomorrow." The hopeful Marcus and the incredulous Silvanus followed Jason into the house.

XXII

"Lazarus, Come Forth!"

EARLY the next morning, as the sun had just risen above the wilderness of Judea, its rays lighting the house-tops of the ancient town, Rebecca stood by the window that faced the caravan road which followed a winding course past the house on to Jericho. She was wide awake despite the long hours of a sleepless night. As the cool morning breeze coming through the open window brought a refreshing glow to her face, Rebecca anxiously awaited the promised arrival of the Master at the home of Mary and Martha.

What would this day bring to her? she asked herself. Would it transport her to raptures of joy or cast her into the depths of misery and despair? "O Lord," she whispered, hardly conscious of what she said, "give Dara the faith and humble heart of the woman of Tyre, and cause him to know that Thou, and Thou alone, art his help."

Looking intently in the direction of Martha's home, she was puzzled to observe a heavily veiled woman who was just leaving the house. Presently she realized that it was Martha and that she seemed to be in a very great hurry. At first Rebecca thought that Martha was hurrying to her brother's tomb, but it was soon plain that she was coming down the road to meet someone. Rebecca was about to leave her place at the window when the sound of many voices came to her ears. In another moment she saw that Jesus, accompanied by a small crowd of excited and curious people, was coming to meet Martha, who had hurried to welcome Him. Her heart

trembling, Rebecca hastened from the room to tell her
friends of the Master's approach.

In her eagerness to see Him, Martha had decided not to
wait until He came, but to meet Him on the way. As
Martha came near, she fell to her knees before Him.
"Martha!" was the Master's only greeting, but it was enough
to relieve her sadness. The look in His eyes, which reflected
merciful understanding of all her troubles, encouraged her
to say in a voice of deep regret and gentle reproach, "O
Lord, if only Thou hadst been here, my brother would not
have died!"

Those of the bystanders who were near enough to hear
began to press closer. One of them, a tall, black-bearded
fellow, his swarthy head covered with a dirty headcloth
and with a tattered woolen plaid slung over powerful brown
shoulders, seemed amused at the woman's cry of sorrow.
Turning to his companion, he said, "I should like to know
what that Man could have done to prevent the death of
Lazarus. No one can resist the cold hand of death nor return
the dead to life again."

The man spoken to was of slight build, and his thin,
misshapen hand was pressed to his throat to stop the painful
fit of coughing which almost exhausted him. But when he
did not succeed immediately, the pitying glance from the
dark eyes of the blackbeard showed that he understood, and
he waited patiently for the cough to subside. "Do not doubt
His power, O Silas," the sick man was finally able to say, "He
surely would have come and done something for Lazarus,
had He known about his sickness."

"My good Reuben," the big fellow replied, "you are ever
willing to find an excuse for another's faults. And I am sorry
to tell you that you are wrong this time, for the Galilean did
know about the sickness of Lazarus. My own ears heard the

message brought to him at Peraea by the woman's messenger who told him about His friend Lazarus."

The sick man found no immediate answer to these words; he only bowed his head as if to hide the look of disappointment that showed in his blurred eyes. The blackbeard, noting his brother's sad look, said, "It is of no use, my brother, to follow this Man much longer. He will not listen to your cry for mercy, and your condition is becoming worse. Let us go as the priest advised you and bathe in the pool of Bethesda, when the water is moved, and perhaps you will get well again."

With unshaken confidence in the power of the Man whose help he sought, Reuben resumed his defense of the Master and said, "If He knew of the sickness of Friend Lazarus, and did not respond to the woman's call at once, I know it was because He had a good reason for His delay."

Before Silas could reply to his brother's assertion, he heard Jesus say, "Martha, thy brother shall rise again."

Unable to comprehend the veiled meaning of these words, Martha replied, "Yea, my Lord, I know that he will rise again in the resurrection of the last day."

"Martha," the gentle voice replied, "I am the Resurrection and the Life; he that believeth in Me, though he were dead, yet shall he live. Believest thou this?"

Reuben's hollow, feverish eyes were filled with wonder as he heard the kneeling woman confidently declare, "Yea, Lord, I believe that Thou art the Christ, the Son of God who has come into the world. And I know that even now whatever Thou wilt ask of the Father, the Father will give it to Thee."

Martha was eager to add more, but Jesus interrupted her by saying, "Tell Mary that I desire to see her."

Her heart filled anew with a feeling of peace, she rose from her knees and hastened away to do as the Master had bidden her.

She found her sister in the garden. Jason and Rebecca and their Roman friends were with her. She at once told her sister of the Master's wish. Mary departed immediately, leaving her friends with Martha, who responded gratefully to their expression of sympathy. Then her own heart was moved to profound pity when she saw the crippled Dara seated on a chair by the rose arbor. For the sorrowful Leonia, who was standing by his side, she had a word of consolation and sympathy. "Do not despair, my dear. I am sure the Master will take from you this sorrow. Now let us be gone, for the Master is tarrying for us by the wayside."

Silvanus lifted Dara to the back of Adallo. Jason, whose face belied his years of suffering, followed, leading blind David by the hand. Marcus and Leonia, together with Martha and Rebecca, completed the little procession as it made its way out of the town to the tomb of Lazarus. The whole town seemed to have assembled there. Men and women, also groups of children, had come from all directions, for the news of the Messiah's arrival had spread like fire throughout the little community, and everyone was eager to get a glimpse of the famous Galilean.

A few feet from the crowd Silvanus halted Adallo and waited for his friends to come up. Dara, excited by the event he hoped to witness presently, for a moment forgot his own infirmity. "Give me your hand," he exclaimed to his friend, standing quietly by the head of the stallion. Before the bewildered centurion realized what was happening, Dara slid from the back of his mount, only to crumple in a heap at the feet of the gray-haired soldier.

"Foolish boy!" Silvanus exclaimed, more alarmed than angry as he picked Dara up with his strong arms. He did not dare say more as he saw the look of disappointment in his young friend's eyes. His own thought was that Dara was not yet ready for the healing hand of the Lord. A passageway was now opened for him as he made his way with Dara through the crowd, enabling him to move closer to the side of Jesus, who was standing before the tomb of Lazarus.

Putting Dara down on the ground with his face toward Jesus, the old soldier stood motionless, and the two men listened attentively to the words of the Lord, who had begun to speak. His eyes rested on the tomb, which was shaded by several olive trees, its entrance sealed with a roughly hewn slab of sandstone.

"Take ye away the stone," Jesus said with a gentle but commanding voice which silenced any objection from those who stood around. However, Martha, who was kneeling by the Lord's side interposed. "No, my Lord, by this time he stinketh. Four days ago my brother died!" His reply was stern but gentle as He looked down at her. "Said I not unto thee that, if thou believest, thou shouldst behold the glory of God?"

The eyes of the three centurions hung on the lips of Jesus. Supreme peace and power seemed to flow from Him as He stood silent for a moment, then said, "Father, I thank Thee that Thou hast heard Me; and because of the people who stand near Me, I said this, that they might believe that Thou hast sent Me."

"What does He mean, Marcus?" Silvanus whispered to his friend. "Who is this Father? And for what purpose has this Father sent Him? It does not make sense to me. According to the story of Rebecca, His father is a humble carpenter from the town of Nazareth in Galilee."

"I know, my friend," Marcus answered, somewhat embarrassed by the question, "it all seems strange to me also. But let us listen."

Jesus spoke again, His voice ringing clear and forceful in the quiet of the morning. "Lazarus, come forth!"

Every eye centered on the open grave and came to rest on the body of Lazarus as it lay stretched on a stone slab. And as they saw him move and rise from the tomb, some were filled with wonder, others with fear. Panic seized the superstitious as they beheld the shrouded figure standing in the entrance, and they would have fled had not the voice of Jesus allayed their panic when He said, "Loose him and let him go."

The two sisters, too astonished to speak, rose from their knees. Both had been convinced of the Lord's power, and yet, when they saw it manifested in the restoration of their brother, they were completely overwhelmed.

Mary, who was first to overcome her shock of emotion, rushed to the side of her brother. With hands that shook with joyous nervousness, the two women began to remove from him the layers of linen that covered his body. And as the napkin that bound his head was removed, they beheld a face radiating the vigor of a new life.

XXIII

"Thou Art Not a Roman"

MARCUS and Silvanus looked down at Dara, a look of surprise and wonder written in their faces. Their minds could not grasp the meaning of what had just taken place before their eyes. It did not seem possible that any man, regardless of his power, could make the dead come to life again. Yet as they beheld the joy of the sisters, with their arms around the shoulders of their brother, they could not dispel the feeling that they had little cause for doubt and uncertainty.

A joyous thrill swept through the multitude as the shock of surprise and wonder at the miracle subsided. Presently the infirm in body as well as those distressed in soul besought the Master for help for their own afflictions. The coughing Reuben, looking earnestly at his brother, said, "Come, Silas, help me to get closer to the Master, that He may hear me. I know He will help me if I call upon Him."

When Silas saw the smile and the expression of peace in his brother's face, he felt ashamed of his own doubt and unbelief. "O Reuben, your faith will make you well," was all he said as tears of bitter regret gave solemn proof of his changed attitude.

Jason, who was deeply interested as he watched the two brothers, momentarily forgot the sad plight of his blind friend. Somewhat embarrassed at the lapse, he turned quickly to David, took him gently by the arm, and said, "Come, David, let us go and beseech the Master's blessing."

"It is the voice of my King that I hear," the blind herder

responded. Jason stood with bated breath as he beheld his
friend, no longer walking with the tentative step of a blind
man, moving confidently toward the Lord without the aid
of the stout cedar staff that now lay discarded on the ground.
A slight tremor passed through the herder's body as his
outstretched hands touched the Lord's garment. Sinking
silently to his knees, he lifted his sightless eyes to the face
above him, unaware that his own son was being carried
beside him by the two centurions.

Cries of protest came from some in the crowd when they
saw Dara. "Away with the Roman! Let him take his ills
to his own people!"

When Dara heard the angry cries, he confessed to himself
that there was some justification for their anger. "It doesn't
seem right," he admitted, "a Roman seeking the help and
mercy of a Jew!"

Turning his eyes to the blind man kneeling by his side,
Dara realized that he had never before had such a close view
of the pale, waxlike face that reminded him of death. The
marks of suffering and untold agony on the features of the
old man so aroused his pity and sympathy that he could not
resist placing his hands gently over the closed eyes of the
blind man. As he did so, Dara did not notice that Jesus was
approaching, and he looked up startled when he heard
Jesus say, "O David, let thine eyes again behold the light
of day, and let eternal darkness be removed from them."

David slowly opened his heavy-lidded eyes, which were
beaming with wonder and thankfulness as they gazed into
the benign face of the Savior. "My Lord and my King!" he
whispered softly with trembling lips, knowing intuitively
that it was He, and his tears fell to the sandaled feet of
the Master.

Not a sound came from the multitude as they stood watching. Jason for a moment acted like one who had lost his reason. But when he recovered sufficiently to realize that David was no longer blind, he drew closer and bent over him, his whole being aquiver with tense expectancy. Had the miracle of healing also restored clarity of mind? Had the clouds in his mind been completely dispelled? Would he recognize an old friend? His racing, incoherent thoughts were suddenly jammed when David, looking hard into his anxious face and hesitating only a moment to fully assure himself, flung both arms around the broad shoulders of the herder and cried, "Nathan, O Nathan, you are alive!" For some minutes the two friends stood in silent embrace, both shaken with deep emotion.

The succession of miracles left Dara so awed and confused that it all seemed unreal to him. Lazarus, who had lain dead in his tomb, had come back to life; and now David, who only a short time ago was the picture of utter helplessness, was standing and embracing the friend of his childhood, his blind eyes healed and his mental vision restored. And why? How had this all come to pass?

Deep down in the young man's heart was the feeling that he knew the reason for it all. They had believed in Him and in His divine power. Drops of perspiration appeared on his forehead as he tried to gather his thoughts and resolve the conflict of loyalties in his own heart. His tortured mind was unable to come at once to a desicion. "I swore allegiance to Caesar only," he said to himself as he nervously considered his dilemma. "How can I pay homage to this Man also? I would then not be loyal to either one."

In his desperation his eyes sought Rebecca for help and comfort, and to his surprise he found her standing close by his side. The glance from her moist eyes told him more than he had ever hoped for. It promised him a life filled with love, health, and contentment, if. . . . He thought for a moment, struggling for something conclusive. "But I do believe in Him! I do believe in Him! But I dare not say it."

"Dara," the girl pleaded, "let not this precious moment pass. To postpone your right decision will mean a life of misery and regret for both of us."

"Nay, nay," the boy cried as he looked into the loving face of the girl, "I do not want to cause you any unhappiness. But what am I to do? His mercy is only for the Jews, and not for me, a Roman!"

Silvanus, Marcus, and Leonia, standing near enough to hear the young couple, looked at one another with questioning glances as they observed Rebecca's anguish at Dara's painful indecision. Jason also heard and stepped quickly to Dara's side, at the same time imploring Jesus, who was about to depart from Bethany. "Lord," the herder said in an appealing voice, "this man believes he can expect no help in his affliction. He thinks he is a Roman, but he is not—a—Roman!"

The Master answered softly, "I know what moves thy heart, O Nathan." And turning to Dara, Jesus said, "Jonathan, behold the face of thy father David, and believe."

Through Dara's paralyzed limbs there began to flow renewed strength as he felt the power of Jesus' eyes upon him. Doubtfully flexing the muscles of his legs to test them, he found with rapturous delight that every muscle responded to his will. Rebecca, near him, cried out with joy, "O Dara, the grace of the Master has made you well again."

Dara could not at once respond to the glad words of the girl, for every fiber of his body and mind was too filled with the blessing which had just been bestowed upon him. But his heart burst forth in singing, "I am well again! And all because of the compassion of the Lord, who saw my suffering!" Vainly the young man tried to find words to express his gratitude. But words were not necessary, for Jesus knew that Dara's heart belonged henceforth to Him.

Leonia, looking at the Lord in speechless wonder, was unable to express the feeling that welled up in her heart when she saw Dara rise briskly to his feet. And before anyone could stop her, she was kneeling at the feet of the Master, pressing the hem of His garment to her lips.

Marcus would have kneeled at her side, but he was deterred by a forbidding glance in Silvanus' eyes. His friend looked angry and defeated. All his pride and vainglory of being a Roman had been crushed by the power of this humble Galilean whom the simple mind of the soldier could not comprehend.

Jesus turned slowly away from them to resume His interrupted journey to Ephraim, leaving behind a little group of people filled with joy and thankfulness. As they stood at the open tomb, excitedly reviewing the miracles of the eventful day, some of the multitude followed the Master, and others hastened to Jerusalem to inform His enemies of His marvelous misdeeds.

XXIV

Bonds of Love

For a long while David and Dara looked at each other in suppressed rapture. Memories of the time when he had last seen his son in Elizabeth's arms were rushing through David's mind. However, with his great delight at seeing his son again there was mingled the sad memory of Elizabeth, who was not at his side to share the joy with him. No longer distressed by the bar of race that had hitherto inhibited a fervent avowal of his deep affection for Rebecca, Dara's heart thrilled with new life, a life which now seemed filled with richness and promise. Forever banished was the fear that for the sake of Roman pride he would be obliged to forfeit all that could make life sweet and dear for him. He now knew that all the wealth of mighty Rome could not bring such true and abiding happiness.

Many times in the past it had been the tender voice of the girl with all the purity and hopefulness of youth that had given him courage and hope, and now, looking into her moist eyes as she leaned on her father's arm, another great joy came to life within him, the joy of the realization that nothing could now prevent their being united in the eternal bond of love.

There had been moments, before he knew of his parentage, when he vaguely felt he wanted to be a Jew. And now that this had come to pass, David was no longer a stranger to him; he was his father. The strong urge of love and of blood caused him to open his arms and embrace the aged man who had been recalled from the unremembered past.

As Leonia, crying softly on the shoulder of her husband, observed the warm embrace of the two men, there flashed suddenly through her mind the alarming thought that she and Marcus would now, to keep their promise to Elizabeth, be obliged to relinquish Dara to the stronger claims of David, his real father, if he decided to hold them to their pledge. Shocked by the eventuality, Leonia was overwhelmed by a loneliness greater than any she had ever before experienced, and the understanding Marcus gently placed his arms around her trembling shoulders as his wife hid her face against his manly bosom.

"Mother dear," Dara pleaded, obviously sensing the cause of Leonia's tears, "why those foolish tears? They are shed for nought. Finding my real father after he was lost to me these many years does not make me less a son of yours and dear Marcus. I shall love and own you both as my parents as long as I shall live. I know that David my father would want it to be so."

It was the stern, serious Jason who answered, "Son, at the hour of your birth, your father and mother bestowed upon you the name of Jonathan, and I indeed rejoice to find you worthy of that noble name. You are indeed a gift from the Almighty. It makes me truly happy to hear you speak so thoughtfully and tenderly of those who took the place of the parents whom Providence had denied you."

On their way back to the house, Rebecca, her eyes filled with tears, bestowed a sudden kiss on the hand of her father, whose warm and tender smile in response to her display of affection showed that he understood the motive which prompted it.

Silvanus, observing all this, felt decidedly ill at ease. It was not that he could not rejoice with David and Dara in their happiness. No, it was not that. Neither was it a want of friendly interest in the romance of Dara and Rebecca. Attempting to analyze his disturbed state of mind, he found that it was rather a consciousness of difference between the others and himself. He discovered a feeling of growing estrangement toward Leonia and Marcus, who, though thoroughly Roman, had readily accepted the so-called Master. But he could not so lightly transfer his fealty. His Roman background and his strong sense of loyalty to her imperial traditions seemed to be an insuperable obstacle which Leonia and Marcus, in his opinion, did not regard with due respect and reverence. On the other hand, he had to admit to himself that his friends, so far as he could see, had lost little and gained much by their new allegiance. Furthermore (and this it was that troubled him most), he had in an unguarded moment of high emotion given Marcus a solemn promise concerning the Galilean. Could he, without violating his code of honor, keep his word to Marcus? It was this last consideration that made him silent, for he realized that a final decision could not be delayed much longer.

No one in the room seemed to notice the brooding soldier, for David was speaking, telling with fascinating realism of his last hours before Herod. "The sight of my father as he lay on the floor, his body pierced by the lance, yet defying the hated monster to the last, made me bear the agonizing hours of torture at the hand of the henchman Ja'bes. I would not tell! I remained faithful to the promise I had given to my father. What happened to me throughout the long years before the noble Cornelius took pity on me I do not know, nor have I any desire to know. Gratitude to my Lord and Redeemer for the boundless mercies shown unto me now fills my heart."

So engrossed were they all with David's account and with other memories of yesterday, that they had not noticed the

approach of night until Rebecca left the room for a moment
to get a small lamp whose flickering flame threw grotesque
shadows on the whitened walls of the room.

Dawn was not far off when they finally retired to seek
some hours of rest. But sleep did not come to their weary
eyes, for their minds were still in wakeful contemplation of
the marvels of the Master's day at Bethany.

The following morning Silvanus was still in a state of indecision. He knew that he would soon have to decide between Caesar and the Man of Galilee. Marcus, reading his
friend's thoughts, decided not to press him. Time and events
in God's keeping, he believed, would compel the decision
without his intervention or assistance.

The three soldiers spent the morning hours in preparing
for their return to Antonia. When the hour of departure
came, Leonia was ready to go with them, and the others
stood at the gate to bid them farewell. Rebecca's hand
trembled on the arm of her father when she saw Dara
untying the reins of the impatient Adallo. Her heart ached
to know what Dara's parting word would be. He did not
leave her long in anxious doubts. For a moment he stood
and looked at her. Then he dropped the reins and came
shyly toward her.

The two young people became suddenly conscious that
every eye was centered on them. And as each read the
thoughts of the other, the young soldier took the unresist-
ing hand of the girl gently into his own and with her knelt
before the noble Jason. Dara, looking up into the loving face
of the old herder, said, "Grant us your blessing, O Jason,
that we both may taste of the joy and happiness that love has
kindled in our hearts. Once I thought it impossible to ask
this blessing of you, but the Master, by whose mercy I was
healed, has vouchsafed this blessing to us."

As Leonia saw them on their knees at Jason's feet, she could not control her emotions. Stooping down beside them, she silently pressed her tearful face to Dara's cheek while through her mind there flashed the memories of their happy years together. Then turning quickly to Rebecca, she kissed her softly on the forehead and whispered, "My dear, do make him happy, for he is indeed the worthy son of the noble David."

Still looking up into Jason's face, Dara was wondering at his silence. He could not know the depth of the emotion surging in the herder's breast who at long last saw his lifelong wish and hope fully realized. "Son," Jason finally said, "the tears of joy shed by Leonia I deem the greatest blessing for you and my beloved child. May the Lord, and the desire to please Him all the days of your life, be ever with you both."

At high noon, under the burning sun three soldiers galloping abreast churned up a cloud of dust that seemed maliciously determined to obscure them from the straining eyes of their friends and lovers, choked in eloquent silence as they lingered at the gate, unwilling to return to a painfully empty house.

XXV

Blest Be the Tie

THE happy days that followed in Jason's little cottage were brought to an abrupt end with the tragic news that Jesus had been taken prisoner by order of Caiaphas, the high priest. Hoping to find some way to effect His release, David, Jason, and Rebecca, together with Lazarus and his sisters traveled to Jerusalem, where they found Marcus and his family equally distressed by the Lord's arrest. Marcus had succeeded in obtaining the promise of the Procurator, Pontius Pilate, that Jesus would be set free. For a while he was hopeful. All, however, seemed lost when a servant brought the message that Pilate, in a futile attempt to extricate himself from a perplexing dilemma, had liberated Barabbas, the murderer, but had condemned the Lord to an ignominious death by crucifixion. Only Lazarus remained firm in the belief that these things were done according to divine design—that the Son must die to restore the fellowship of fallen man with God.

The others, unable to comprehend the full significance of the words of Lazarus, were unwilling to rest until they were certain that they could do nothing to save Him from that terrible fate. Even Silvanus, who as yet could not find it in his heart to accept Christ as the true Son of God—even he refused to believe it was too late to help. But their importunate pleading fell on deaf ears, and all their efforts were useless. With averted eyes they stood at the cross as He was crucified, —He, who had been a great Friend to so many, friendless in the hour of His greatest need. The Romans, unaware of the appropriate setting, placed His cross between those of the thieves who were crucified with Him. Their last hope gone, His Bethany friends returned sad and desolate to their homes.

On the third day after the dark and frightening event they had witnessed at Golgotha, Silvanus rushed breathlessly to his friends Marcus and Leonia at the Fortress with the stirring news, "The Lord is risen! They have seen him. The tomb is empty!" With the wings of the wind the words flew, almost sooner heard than told, and before long the tidings came to David and Jason and their friends in Bethany. Surely the Master was the Son of God, and all doubt had vanished —even from the troubled Silvanus.

Many months had passed since that eventful Easter morning in Jerusalem. This metropolitan center of Judaism was likewise the base from which the Gospel radiated and spread, adding great numbers to the community of believers, which soon included some Gentiles, among whom were officers and men of the imperial army.

Pilate was rather surprised and disappointed when the three soldiers applied for their release from the service, and upon inquiry as to their reason, Marcus replied rather evasively, "Sir, I have grown old in service of the empire, and I desire to spend the rest of my days in peace and quiet at my estate in Rome. And as for my son, Dara, and the centurion Silvanus, they belong to my family, and I would not like to go without them." The Procurator seemed satisfied with this answer, though Marcus preferred to remain silent about his real motive. He did not tell Pilate of the great change wrought in him by the restoration of Dara and by the other miracles of the Man from Galilee.

As soon as the order for their release came, the soldiers and their families hastened to prepare for their departure from the land where they had experienced the deepest sorrow as well as the greatest happiness. Marcus thanked the doctor, Julian, for his faithful and conscientious years of service. Rebecca sobbed on Mary's bosom as she took leave of the two sisters whom she loved so dearly, while Lazarus, ever a source of inspiration and comfort, earnestly besought God's blessing for his friends.

With all preparations for their departure completed, the little company began their journey, traveling in easy stages in consideration for the comfort of Leonia and Rebecca. Nathan, at first quite averse to joining them, was fully consoled by the prospect of living out his remaining years in the comfortable security of the home which Marcus had promised to provide for Rebecca and her husband.

Arriving finally at the seaport of Caesarea, they stopped at the house of Cornelius. The aged centurion welcomed them joyfully. When he saw the gentle David dismount without the help of his friends, he was filled with astonishment, for he realized that the old herder had regained his sight. Smiling, he looked at Marcus, who had noticed the surprise in his eyes. To the unspoken question of Cornelius, Marcus replied, "Yes, my Cornelius, it is the 'Servant of the King,' and he is well again."

Sometime later, as they dined together, Cornelius listened with avid interest to Marcus as he related the amazing story of the restoration of David and his son. When the long, detailed account was concluded, the centurion bowed his head and said, "The mercies of the Lord are beyond comprehension. But, I too, have seen His wonders."

Whereupon Cornelius, rising from his seat between Marcus and Silvanus, began to relate his own equally astounding experience. "Four days ago I was fasting until this hour, and at the ninth hour I prayed in my house, and behold, a man stood before me in bright clothing and said, 'Cornelius, thy prayer is heard, and thine alms are had in remembrance in the sight of God. Send therefore to Joppa and call hither Simon, whose surname is Peter, who is lodged in the house of one Simon the tanner, by the seaside, who, when he cometh, shall speak unto you.' I did as I was commanded, and I am happy to announce that the Apostle will be here tomorrow."

Cornelius now asked his friends to repair to the atrium, indicating that he wished to speak further with them. At the same time he motioned to his servant Rufus, who appeared at once from his station near the entrance. When Cornelius saw that all were seated, he turned to Marcus and resumed his story. "Once, Marcus," he began, "I promised to tell you how it happened that I became a follower of the Galilean and changed my way of living. When we last met, you remarked about the change that had occurred, but you did not know the reason. Since you and Silvanus and I have been close friends for many years, I shall speak quite freely. Together we often paid our tributes to the gods—not that we trusted very much in their power to keep us from harm, but it was the custom for good citizens to do so. We were separated when I was transferred to Caesarea to assume command of the Italian Band that is in garrison here. Throughout all these years, my loyal Rufus," with a friendly nod to his servant, "never left my side. He was indispensable to me, a servant with the privileges of a close friend.

"About ten years after I came to Caesarea, I began to notice that a great change had taken place in Rufus. As you may recall, and I hope he will pardon the reference to his past, he had always been a rather boisterous, intemperate fellow. However, one day, much to my surprise, he refused to pledge me in a cup of wine. Later he refused to go with me to sacrifice to the gods. I did not immediately press him for an explanation. Neither did I upbraid him for his strange conduct.

"A few months later, as I was strolling in the moonlight, I came upon Rufus kneeling near the Court of Swans in an attitude of prayer. I thought him drunk, but he explained, 'I have been praying, O master, to the only God who is able to help me and to grant me the mercies of which I am so greatly in need'."

Rufus now asked permission to continue the story himself. "It was in the course of a conversation that I had with a poor Hebrew slave that I saw a new purpose in life. This slave told me a wondrous story of a Man from Galilee, named Jesus, who walked and preached among His people and taught them to love one another and to worship the only true God. He also told me of the wondrous works wrought by this Man among all the people. It was to Him that my master saw me praying that night in the court."

Laying his hand warmly on the old servant's shoulder, Cornelius said, "My friends, from that time, I, too, have been a changed man. Many times since, have I gone with him to the fountain to watch the glorious stars in the heavens and to worship the everlasting God. And many times have I knelt with him, beseeching this God Eternal to give me the peace and happiness my restless soul had ever longed for."

After Cornelius had finished, his friends withdrew to their rooms for the night, each heart filled to overflowing with elation.

The following morning, at the sound of the bronze gong at the main gate, Cornelius and his friends hastened to the door. The old soldier bowed his knees in an attitude of worship when he saw that it was Peter the Apostle. But the disciple took his hand and said, "Cornelius, stand up, for I am only a man like yourself."

A short time later, Peter beheld the people assembled

before him in the spacious library. He began to speak. "By the Law of Moses it is unlawful for a man who is a Jew to keep company with one of another nation. All the years of my life I have invariably observed this ordinance. However, by a special vision God has taught me that I should not call any man common or unclean. Therefore I came unto you without gainsaying as soon as I was sent for.

"Unto me is revealed a great truth. I perceive that God is no respecter of persons, but that in every nation he that feareth Him and worketh righteousness is acceptable to Him."

Slowly, with a fascinating simplicity, the Apostle spoke of God, and of His love, and told how God had sent His only Son to die to redeem His people of Israel. "But they refused Him," Peter cried out, filled with the spirit of the moment. "Yea, they slew Him, the Prince of Peace, and hanged Him on a tree! But He arose again on the third day. And I am a witness to this and speak the truth, for I sat at meat with Him and many of His brethren after He was risen from the dead. And now I am commanded to preach His Gospel of salvation, that whosoever believeth in Him shall have eternal life."

When some of the assembled Jews saw that the Gentiles followed Peter's words with believing hearts, they were astounded. They had believed that faith in Jesus and His salvation was a prerogative reserved exclusively for Abraham's children. When Peter concluded after a few minutes, the members of the household and the guests were inspired with a new hope. Even Silvanus, no longer resisting or doubtful, bowed his head in solemn thanksgiving.

When Marcus and his party boarded a Rome-bound ship at the port of Caesarea, Peter and Cornelius stood at the wharf to bid them farewell. As the ship left its mooring to sail into the Mediterranean mist, Peter's parting words of exhortation seemed still to hang in the silent morning air.

"Be ye faithful and worthy of the vocation wherein ye are called, that ye testify for the Lord Jesus who has wrought such wonderful things in you."

"We will remember," answered the gentle David. "And if the Master willeth it, ye shall hear of this our testimony."

Date Due

Mr 28 47			
DEC 5 '47			
Jan. 7			
OCT 11 '48			
OCT 25 '48			
APR 11 '49			
APR 11 '49			
MAY 20 '49			
FEB 17 '50			
DEC 4 '51			
FEB 23 '52			
APR 8 1954			
NOV 26 1954			
DEC 10 1954			
JAN 5 1958			
JUL 12 1958			
FEB 14 '62			
FEB 28 '62			